Standard Hollywood Depravity

BY ADAM CHRISTOPHER

STANDARD Hollywood DEPRAVITY

ADAM CHRISTOPHER

A TOM DOHERTY ASSOCIATES BOOK

NEW YORK

STANDARD HOLLYWOOD DEPRAVITY

Copyright © 2017 by Seven Wonders Ltd.

Cover art and design by Will Staehle

Edited by Miriam Weinberg

A Tor.com Book

Published by Tom Doherty Associates

175 Fifth Avenue

New York, NY 10010

www.tor.com

Tor® is a registered trademark of Macmillan Publishing Group, LLC.

ISBN 978-0-7653-9182-7 (ebook)
ISBN 978-0-7653-9183-4 (trade paperback)

First Edition: March 2017

For Sandra, always

You ask me how anybody can survive Hollywood?
Well, I must say that I personally had a lot of fun there.
—Raymond Chandler
November 7, 1951

ACKNOWLEDGMENTS

They say that what happens in Saratoga Springs, stays in Saratoga Springs. Only on this particular occasion I find myself obliged to break with the rules of late-night bar chat, because this novella owes its very existence to one of those random moments that are undoubtedly the best bits of any convention. In this instance it was World Fantasy 2015, where Tor.com's Associate Publisher Irene Gallo and I hatched a plan to expand the Raymond Electromatic Mysteries beyond a series of three books (which start, incidentally, with *Made to Kill* and continue on to *Killing is My Business*). And who was I to argue? I'd already started this whole shebang with a novelette, "Brisk Money," written for *Tor.com* back in 2014. *Standard Hollywood Depravity* felt like coming home.

My thanks then to Irene and the whole team at Tor.com who work very, very, very hard making writers like me look good—Lee Harris, Mordecai Knode, and Katharine Duckett. Thanks also to editor Miriam Weinberg and to cover designer extraordinaire Will Staehle, who (at the time of writing) has designed and covered an extraordinary nine of the twelve books I've had published, and he only didn't do the other three because they were tie-ins. Lucky doesn't even begin to describe how I feel about that particular statistic.

Literary superagent Stacia J. N. Decker of Dunow, Carlson & Lerner helped get this novella into shape with her extraordinary eye, for which I remain forever grateful.

And finally, thanks to my wife, Sandra, who continues to amaze me with her love, support, and encouragement. This novella is for you.

Standard Hollywood Depravity

1

The story of how I came to meet a girl called Honey started late on a fall Tuesday night when I was nursing a scotch and watching girls dance in a nightclub that was named after both of those things.

The fact that I couldn't drink the scotch didn't matter much to me. Nor did it matter much to the man behind the bar. I just kept the glass in front of me, sometimes sliding it a few inches across the dark and greasy wood into my left hand, sometimes a few inches in the opposite direction, and so long as I occasionally put a two-dollar bill folded lengthways somewhere near the glass, the man behind the bar was happy enough to occasionally relieve me of it. On top of all that I was keeping myself tucked away in the corner. It seemed only polite, seeing as I was six feet and something more of bronzed steel-titanium alloy that filled out a tan-colored trench coat the same way a '64 Plymouth Fury filled out the parking bay of a narrow suburban garage.

Not that I felt conspicuous. This seemed to be my lucky night for going undercover, which was something I rarely did on account of the fact that I was not only a robot but the *last* robot, which tended to make me stick out in a crowd just somewhat.

But not here and not tonight, because there was a band playing in the club and they were pretty good too, not only at playing what they were playing but at commanding the attention of the club's clientele. This was on account of the fact that the band was five handsome boys from across the pond with hair that looked long enough to be annoying in the morning and suits that seemed to shine under the lights and voices that were polished with an accent that people in this country seemed to like, and quite a lot too. They played on the stage at the back of the room that stood maybe two feet higher than the dance floor. I wondered if they were famous. I wouldn't know. But they looked cute and the beat was strong and steady and the girls in the big bird cages suspended from the ceiling right over the dance floor were doing their level best to keep up. There were four of them and they were a mass of swinging limbs and shaking heads and tassels that shimmied like an alpine waterfall.

Business as usual for a club like this.

Except this didn't seem like a usual night. Sure, the club was packed and most of those squeezed around tables that were too small to put anything really useful on were as thin and as young and as cute as the band on the stage. They were the kind of kids who lived on tobacco smoke and drinks made out of gin and vermouth and a twist of lime and who liked to go out in nice clothes and shake those clothes to the sound of music.

For a moment I felt old and then for another moment I wondered whether this particular feeling was something I'd inherited from Professor Thornton. I couldn't be certain, but I was fairly sure this would not have been his kind of party.

Among those drinking and those moving to the beat underneath the dancing girls, sure, I was out of place.

But I wasn't the only one. I would even go so far as to say I was one of many.

At the back of the club, away from the lights, in the dark where the cigarette smoke floated thickest, were scattered a bunch of men. These men all wore suits and coats and their hats stayed firmly where they had been placed. These men were all of a build and disposition that suggested work done in darkness and behind closed doors, work that was messy and wet and not something you told your friends about. My logic gates told me that the way the men sat hunched and silent and immobile at the back tables and at the bar stools near my own little dark corner suggested that they were not in fact here for a night on the town. They were all here for something else entirely.

Just like me, in fact. So no, I didn't feel out of place, not in the slightest.

I slid my glass from one hand to the other and watched as, like me, the men didn't drink the drinks that were sitting in front of them. What they did do was smoke. The air was thick with it. My clothes were going to need to be laundered after this and not just to get rid of the bloodstains.

I watched the men and for a moment there I entertained the notion that maybe I wasn't the last robot in the world after all. But then a lug in a suit a half size too small, with a hat a half size too big drooping low over a brow his Neanderthal ancestors would have been proud of, snorted as he kept watch on the rest of his friends and then poked a finger into the problem nostril and had a good rummage around.

So he was human enough. Robots didn't have sinus problems, although as I watched him out of the corner of my optics, for a second I swore there was an itch somewhere in the middle of my faceplate and for another second, I had an image of a man in a tweed jacket pulling a striped handkerchief out of an overstuffed pocket and giving his nose a good one.

And then it was gone and I looked back down at my scotch and I saw that the barman had made another withdrawal from the bank of the Electromatic Detective

Agency. I looked up but he had moved somewhere else. What was in front of me now was the mirror at the back of the bar. It ran the whole length and it showed me the room and myself pretty well. I noticed that the top button of my trench coat had come undone. I did it up. It was a little tight. Then there was another movement in the mirror.

To get into the main room of the club you walked through a set of swinging double doors. The doors were behind me and now they swung and I watched in the mirror as another young couple waltzed right in.

He was thin and young and blond and had cheekbones to die on a hillside for and a firm mouth just built for kissing. She was more of the same. Together the lovely pair paused at the threshold. I wondered if he was going to carry her over it. Then she looked around and nodded at something and they headed for almost the only table that wasn't otherwise engaged, a small circular number like all the rest in the joint that was positioned right on the dance floor's eastern front. As they moved to it, the men watched them move and I watched the men. I think the boy noticed their audience by the way he fixed the smile on his face and kept his eyes on his lady friend as he held the chair out for her. If she noticed anything was wrong with this scene she didn't show it. She was here for a good time and already her blond bob was swaying to the beat and her eyes were on the go-go dancers above and the mass of bodies twisting on the floor below.

I frowned on the inside and switched my scotch from my left hand to my right. The couple were fine, exactly the right kind of cute for the club, the same as all the others, and yet they worried me and I didn't know why and that worried me some more. Maybe it was because the boy looked nervous. Maybe it was because the girl didn't seem to notice.

I thought about this and then I thought about it some more as the young couple at the table leaned into each other. She was saying something and whatever he was saying back she didn't like because now the sway of her bob was to a different rhythm. I imagined he was telling her he wanted to leave. He'd seen the heavies at the back of the room and he didn't like them and I didn't blame him.

And given what I had to do that evening I wished she would take his advice.

Her and all the others.

A moment later she pulled back and shook her head and then he pulled back and frowned and then she got up and went onto the dance floor. So much for that. The other kids dancing made room for her and soon enough she found a nice spot near the stage. Then she bent her arms at the elbows, bent her legs at the knee, and started shaking herself around to the beat. The band noticed and picked up a little and the guy in the front spun around on the toes of one of his Cuban heels. Everyone seemed to like this, and in another few moments everyone in club was watching the girl show what she could do.

Everyone in the club except the boyfriend, who was too busy working on his frown and too busy studying the grain of his little round table.

One of the go-go dancers bent down in her cage and moved her arms around like she was beckoning to the girl to come up and join her. The girl down below laughed and moved closer and the two of them began to dance together at separate altitudes.

I watched the pair dance and I thought about the job I was here for and my optics moved up from the girl on the floor to the one up in the cage. I assumed she was a good dancer on account of the fact that the establishment was willing to pay her to dance for hours at a time. I had to admit that dancing was not something my circuits could get a grip on. It seemed like a lot of effort to oscillate in time to a beat and all everyone seemed to be doing was getting sweaty and out of breath.

Maybe that was part of the appeal.

I turned my attention back to the crowd in the club. Couples were now peeling off the dance floor, eager for refreshment, faces alight with smiles and laughter and lips already twitching in anticipation of fresh cigarettes. The boyfriend had slumped in his chair, but his eyes were finally on his girl out on the floor.

And the men at the back stayed right where they were. Some of the kids glanced over at them and there were some whispers, but other than that nobody seemed to think much was wrong. It was a free country and if you wanted to wear your overcoat to a bar while you didn't drink anything that was entirely your business and nobody else's.

I thought about this for a moment. Then I thought about this again.

I adjusted my hat and tried to sink into the shadows by the bar. I was starting to get a feeling I knew what was going on and what kind of business the men were here for. It was a sinking kind of feeling that materialized just under my pan-neural charge coil. I didn't like it much.

The men were muscle. Pure and simple. They were goons and gangsters, mobsters, hoods. Thugs, garden variety, and they weren't dancing because they weren't here to dance and they weren't drinking because their bosses had told them to keep off the sauce.

They were here to watch. To guard the approaches. Maybe their bosses were here too, but not at the bar. Somewhere else. Somewhere behind doors that were closed and guarded by more wide men in big suits.

So sure. I *did* fit right in after all. It was dark in the corner and the club was smoky and like the others I had kept my hat on and pulled down. As far as they knew, I was one of them.

I had to admit, it was a crying shame. Because I wasn't here for them, or their bosses. I did a head count. Must have been every hood in Los Angeles collected together under a single roof. The thought of the potential collars available to me here sent my circuits fizzing. I could clean up LA in a heartbeat, if I had one. All I'd need to do was make a call. Rattle off the number of my private investigator's permit and the boys in blue would have a good night.

Except I wasn't a detective any more. Sure, my license was still valid. It was a good cover. Let me move around places and ask questions without having questions asked back.

But I was here for that other reason. That other job, the one my boss, Ada, had sent me to do.

The job I was programmed to do.

I was here to kill someone.

The person I was here to kill wasn't wearing a suit or a hat and that someone sure wasn't picking his teeth with a toothpick while he leaned against the back of his chair and watched his cigarette smoke ride thermals to the ceiling like the lazy daydream of a sailor lost at sea.

I glanced back at the girl on the dance floor. She was still going for it. So was the go-go dancer in the cage above her. Every now and then she glanced down at the girl and smiled and the girl smiled and they both shimmied and shimmied.

I focused on the girl in the cage. She had black hair that shone and that curled up as it touched her bare shoulders. She wore a small red two-piece outfit that looked like it would be pretty good for swimming in if it wasn't for all the tassels that shook like palm trees in a hurricane. She wore white leather boots that were tight around the calf and that ended just below her knees.

She looked like she was good at her job and she looked like she was enjoying it too.

I knew precisely two things about her.

First, I knew her name was Honey.

Second, I knew she had to die.

2

There was a telephone booth out by the coat check. The payphone was stuck on the wall and there was a half dome of see-through green plastic curved over it. I couldn't fit underneath the dome so I stood next to it. I reached for the phone. Then I turned and looked at the girl at the coat check do her nails as the music thudded from the dance floor beyond the big double doors. Behind the girl I could see a large collection of coats and hats neatly hung, and I knew that none of them belonged to the men at the back of the bar. They needed their coats to hide all their guns and their knives and they needed their hats in place because every crook worth his salt needed a low-pulled brim to peer out from under.

I thought about the men awhile as I stood by the telephone. I hadn't expected them to be here and I didn't like them being around. I was here on a job. Which meant it had to be clean—in and out and no fuss made.

But there was something else going on at the club tonight. That made things less clean. More complicated. Whatever it was that the bad guys were here for I needed to stay out of it. Which was not in itself an unusual proposition because staying out of things was something of a hobby of mine. Sure, it wasn't easy, being the last robot in the world, but I got by. I was just lucky that my being the last robot in the world was, at least as far as I could tell, one of the key reasons why people never put two and two together and came up with an answer about the little enterprise Ada ran out of the office in the building on the corner of Hollywood and Cahuenga.

That, and the fact that I was good at my job. So good they paid me to do it, in fact.

But still, the men in the club were a surprise and surprises were not good for business. I had to call the office and let Ada know about it.

I kept my optics on the coat-check girl while my hand reached under the green dome and grabbed the telephone. I put it against the side of my head and the receiver clicked in my ear and I heard the faint roar of an ocean far away.

"So have you done the twist again," Ada asked, "like you did last week to the neck of that dentist from Des Moines?"

The girl at the coat check glanced up and kept filing her nails without looking. That seemed like quite a skill.

I turned my back on her.

"You'll need to tell me about last week sometime," I said.

"Oops, sorry, Ray. Loose lips sink ships," Ada said, and then she made a sound like those lips were wrapped around the end of a cigarette and taking a healthy draw.

Considering Ada was a computer the size of an office, this image seemed unlikely. But still it was there. Dancing in front of my optics.

And then it was gone.

She kept talking. "Anyway, last week, long story short, once upon a time there was this guy, a dentist, and then, what do you know, he got his neck broke. Someone twisted it the wrong way. Not that there is a right way."

"What was that about loose lips?"

"Hey, can't a girl change her mind?"

I didn't answer. Ada ignored my silence.

"Say, do they still do the Watusi?" she asked—mostly, I suspected, to herself. "I lose track. I don't get out much you see, Raymondo."

"If this is your way of asking whether the deed is done, then you're in for disappointment."

Ada laughed. Two full loops. I counted them both.

And then she said, "The night is young, chief," and then someone in the back of my mind leaned back in the big chair behind my big desk in my small office and put her stockinged feet up on the big desk and watched her own toes wriggle in the dim light from the street that came in through the big window behind her.

And then I said: "Yeah, about that," and as I said it the mirage of someone who might have existed once upon a time but no longer did faded. I felt the voltage change in my positronic calculator. I didn't like the feeling. It was the feeling that something wasn't right.

Ada hummed on the line, or maybe it was just the line itself that hummed. "I don't like it when you say things like that, Ray. What's up?"

I turned back to the coat-check girl and she was still there and still doing her nails and chewing on something but now her eyes were back on her nails and not on me. When I shifted on my feet the coiled cable of the telephone moved with me and it must have made a noise because the coat-check girl stopped what she was doing and looked at me, her jaw only partway through the next chew.

I frowned on the inside and I lowered the phone's mouthpiece and jutted my steel chin in the girl's direction.

"You want to go get yourself a glass of milk or something?"

The girl began to chew again, although more slowly, and one manicured eyebrow went high up on her forehead. She looked like she was too young to remember a time when a robot would have done the job she was doing but for none of the money. Her only knowledge of robots probably came from schoolbooks and a hazy memory of her daddy's breakfast-table complaints about the unemployment rate as he read the early edition over his cornflakes.

She resumed chewing and her eyes moved up and down and all around me with not an atom of interest. But she took the hint and two seconds later slid her nail file into a pocket and then she was gone and I was alone with the hats and the coats and the dull kick of the drums from out on the dance floor.

"There's something else going on here tonight, Ada," I said into the dead telephone. "You know anything about it?"

"What do I ever know, chief?" said Ada. "We got the job. We got our down payment. We got a name and a place and a time and off you went to pay the lucky lady a visit. Now all you need to do is get up close and personal and make sure she doesn't get up close and personal with anyone ever again."

"That's just it."

"What's just it? You don't want to get lipstick on your chassis?"

The drums from the main club room kicked up and I turned to look. I imagined Honey and the other three cage dancers go-go-going for it while the blond girl vibrated underneath them all and everyone else stood and watched and clapped.

The things people do for fun.

"Getting her alone might be difficult. Her work is the kind of work that people pay a cover charge just to sit and watch."

"I know what a go-go dancer is, Ray. Jeez Louise, how old do you think I am?"

I pondered on that question for as long as it took two microswitches somewhere inside me to flip and I pondered what Ada would say if I actually asked her.

"So I get her alone," I said.

"So you get her alone," said Ada. "Well done, Ray, you got the job! The pay is great but the hours are terrible."

"Listen, getting her alone might be difficult. There are people watching her."

"I think I saw the rerun of this conversation last Sunday, Ray."

"What I mean is," I said, "is that she's being watched, and not by the young and lovely of Hollywood out for an after-work sniff or two."

I told her about the men at the back of the bar. I told her about my theory about the men. I told her it made things complicated.

Maybe the big chair in my small office rocked forward on its springs. Maybe it didn't.

Ada didn't speak at first because she inserted a pause as heavy as a ripe pumpkin waiting to be carved for Halloween. Then she spoke.

"Well, there you go," said Ada. "Just your standard Hollywood depravity."

If I could have raised an eyebrow I would have.

"Anything you can find out?" I asked. "Put your ear to the ground, so to speak? Make a call or two?"

"Not sure, chief," said Ada. "We're not supposed to ask questions. I don't *like* asking questions. We get the job and then we get the job done. And so the world keeps turning, whether it's full of hoods listening to music or not. Our business, this isn't."

"I know," I said, "but I'm the one on the ground. The job got difficult. I need information. I need to know what might be going on so I know what I might need to do about it in case things get more difficult."

The noise on the phone line ticked up in volume. And I heard it then, buried in the roar. The ticking of a clock, the second hand of a fast watch curving around and around and around.

The sound of the computer room back at the office.

The sound of *Ada*, the real sound that wasn't someone smoking or drinking coffee or moving things around on my desk.

"Because," I said, "it can't be a coincidence that I've

been sent to rub out Honey tonight of all nights. She must be connected to whatever is going down and that means it's going to get difficult. Difficult is not good. I don't like difficult."

"You have a point there, chief. Maybe I should go back and ask for more money."

There was some yodeling from beyond the doors.

"Is that what young people like to dance to now?" Ada asked.

I shrugged. I glanced up and to the left of the green dome of the phone booth. There was a poster on the wall and my optics scanned it.

"They're called the Hit List. They're from England."

Ada laughed inside my head. "I like the name. And the accent."

I shrugged again and put my back to the racket once more. I preferred it that way. "You want me to put a hold on the job while you make enquiries?"

"You can take five, Ray. But listen, the contract was specific. Has to be tonight."

There was a pause and a click on the line even as Ada finished what she was saying. I thought she was thinking what I was thinking at the same time I was thinking it.

There were no such things as coincidences.

Ada said, "Would help if we had some pictures to help ID the crowd."

"I've taken holiday snaps," I said. I had camera eyes and four rolls of fresh film in my chest.

"*Atta boy*, chief! Wire them to me and I'll rattle some cages. See if I can find out what the party is."

"Okay," I said. "I'll head out to the car and send them over."

Somewhere behind me the music stopped and the singer spoke into the microphone. With his accent it sounded like I'd tuned in to *Masterpiece Theater*.

"Well, there you go," said Ada. "Intermission. You can go get a root beer after you wire me those pictures."

I hung the telephone up. The girl at the coat check was back. There was nobody else around and all that emanated now from beyond the doors of the club was the hum of conversation and the clink of inexpensive glassware.

I jerked a thumb over my shoulder to suggest I was about to head out the main doors, although why I felt the need to suggest that to the coat-check girl I didn't know. It just felt like the right thing to do.

The coat-check girl nodded then pulled the nail file from her pocket and got back to work.

I went outside and headed to where my car was parked.

3

It was a beautiful night. I might have been a robot but you didn't need to tell me when a night was beautiful or not. And this one sure was.

It was late. Heading past eleven, but only just. This was fine. I had power enough for a few hours yet. Back in the old days, midnight really had been the witching hour, the appointed moment when the part of me that I was aware of switched off and the part of me that Ada whispered sweet nothings to switched on. That was when I'd got to work. Private detective by day. Private killer by night.

But Ada had told me, eventually. And that was fine. She was the computer and she could reprogram not just herself but me too. A little adjustment and I was invited to the party.

Which was also fine. Because I was programmed to think it was fine. A robot has to make a living somehow. And I always did my best work after midnight. It seemed tonight would not be an exception.

So it was a beautiful night. It was fall but it was warm and dry. I think they called that an Indian summer, although I don't know why. The club was on the corner of Sunset Boulevard and North Clark Street in West Hollywood. The main doors opened out on the corner and there was a parking lot out the back that you got to via an alley on Clark. I walked up that street and into the lot and then I stopped and looked up. The sky above me was clear. There were a lot of stars and no clouds and no moon either. There was a warm breeze coming in off the sleeping hills to the north and on that breeze came the scent of wild sage and dust and the desert. I might have been a robot but you didn't need to tell me that was the greatest smell in the world.

I got to my car without difficulty. The parking lot was nearly empty, just my Buick and a handful of smaller numbers. None of the cars would have belonged to the hoods in the club so there was no point in checking any of them. The men would have scattered their vehicles all over the neighboring streets.

I was alone, but when I got to my car I still stopped and checked before I slipped in and shut the door with a click as gentle as the first tap of a silver spoon on a soft-boiled egg.

I sat in the car and plugged myself into the dash and began to wire the pictures I'd taken inside the club to Ada. The car had a radio telephone and a number of other toys courtesy of my creator, Professor Thornton.

He'd thought of everything, including the fact that I could scan the negatives directly off the film rolls in my chest and send them back to base. That was a useful trick for a private detective.

The good professor might have been a little disappointed if he'd known the line of work his creations had moved into, but he was dead so disappointment was no longer a concern.

I'd used one of the four rolls of film inside my chest already. I wasn't sure how good the pictures were because the club was dark and smoky and even with my optics turned up to eleven the men in the club had a habit of keeping the brims of their hats down low over their eyes.

Funny that, I thought. Almost as though they didn't want people seeing who they were.

The wirephoto machine in the car was slow but that was fine. I wound down my window and I watched the back of the club. There wasn't much to watch, just a Dumpster and a back door and through the open window came the sounds of Sunset Boulevard and the dull thud of the Hit List starting back up from inside the club and the smell of the hills and then came the sound of something else entirely and the unique smell that went with it.

I reran the audio inside my head to be sure. I tweaked

the equalizer, tried a couple of filters, changed the volume. To be sure.

I was sure.

Then the back door of the club opened and someone stepped out into the parking lot. With no moon it was pretty dark, and the building itself cast an even deeper darkness through which the figure moved. That same darkness hid me in the car as I turned up my optics and took a good look.

The sound had been the sound of a gunshot. Small caliber, quiet. Not silenced, but hidden well under the music. Like someone had timed it. It was lucky my ears were of the electronic variety, otherwise that shot would have been the secret it was supposed to be.

The smell had been the smell of the very same gunshot, and it lingered in the air, faint on the warm breeze and nothing but a tingle of fireworks at the back of the throat. Not that I had a throat, but what I did have was a chemical analyzer with an intake in the middle of my faceplate. An analyzer that had been enjoying the desert scents and had alerted me to the smell of gunpowder as a matter of routine.

The person moving through the dark completed the picture so I sat back and watched. They moved slowly at first, coming out of the back door of the club and shifting like they were looking around, checking to see that the coast was clear. It was. There was nobody back here but me and in the dark I would have been pretty hard to see sitting inside the Buick.

Then the figure moved faster and moved from my left to my right, across the back of the club. On the right side was the Dumpster, which sat against a low wall that separated this particular piece of real estate from the one next door. The person made their way to the Dumpster and lifted the big lid only by a fraction. Their hand went in then came out.

There they stopped and then after a moment they kept on going, vaulting the low wall and making their way toward another alley that ran down that side of the club and that would lead around to the main strip and eventually to the main doors of the club. Maybe that was a clever move. It put them at some distance from whatever it was they'd delivered to the Dumpster and I knew from personal experience there was only the girl at the coat check with any kind of view of the main door—and she didn't have much interest in who came and went. She wouldn't know or even care if someone went out the back then came back in the front.

I was right. Something was happening tonight.

Normally I wouldn't care. Not my problem. I had my job to do. Yes, I wanted more information on what was going on but only to help me do that job. That was why I had called Ada. That was why I was wiring her some pictures. I didn't want things to get difficult.

They'd gotten difficult. Now I did have a problem and that problem had a name.

Honey. The girl I was supposed to kill. The girl who had just fired a gun inside the club and then hidden that gun in the Dumpster before making a quick and agile getaway, tassels swinging.

So I'd been right. Something was happening and Honey was involved. The fact that I was right didn't make me feel any better, but I took what comfort I could from the accuracy of my logic gates anyway.

My eyes fell to the dash of my car. The pictures had gone through so I unplugged and then I opened the door of the car and I got out. I stood there for a moment in that warm breeze. The smell of the gunshot was long gone. I closed the door and then put my hands in my pockets and walked over to the Dumpster. The parking lot was gravel and my footsteps crunched all the way over.

I got to the Dumpster. I was still alone. I lifted the Dumpster's lid. Inside were bags of trash and on top of one of the bags was something small and black.

I reached inside and pulled the gun out and stood there looking at it for a while. It was a little thing, a mouse gun. Small caliber. Looked like a .22. My steel fingers would never even have gotten through the trigger guard.

I closed the lid of the Dumpster and put the gun in my pocket and then turned and headed to the back door of the club. As I reached for that door I wondered who Honey was and why I was supposed to kill her.

These were questions I was not supposed to ask.

But I asked them anyway.

4

The back door of the club led to a corridor, the walls of which were brick that had been painted a sort of purple-red. Maybe you'd call it magenta. The air that came in with me from the parking lot was warm while the air between the brick walls was cool.

There was nobody around so I kept going. The smell of the gun had long since evaporated outside but it was still lingering here. It wasn't anything anybody could have smelled. It had some stiff competition with all the smoke from the club itself. Cigarette mostly. A little cigar. Nothing fancy but enough to smother everything else like a soft pillow.

But my analyzer was working away and I turned the dial up a little until the smell was so strong I could follow it like an airline pilot coming in to land.

Bully for me.

The club was big enough out the back. Lots of storerooms filled with the kinds of things club storerooms are filled with. Booze. Cigarette cartons. Boxes of Christmas decorations that would be excavated soon enough. I kept following my nose. Nothing was locked. The club was running strong and so people needed to get stuff out of the storage rooms. I walked some more, found an office. More storerooms. A big room you could hire out for a private function. This one was empty and had stacks of chairs rising up along the walls.

I figured there would be another room like this one, on the other side of the building. If my guess about what was going on here tonight was anything close to being right, I was betting that other room wasn't empty.

I kept walking and went through a door, and then I found myself out by the coat check again. The door I had just stepped through was on the other side of the cloak-room from the big double doors that led to the dance floor. The coat-check girl had abandoned her post.

The airborne chemical trail led me across the lobby to a set of doors that was across from the telephone booth with its green dome. I took a look at the sign on the doors. Restrooms, male and female. I generated a random number. It came out even so I put a metal palm on the door to the men's. Before I pushed that metal palm I tuned my audio receptors to the void beyond the door, but I couldn't hear anything except the trickle of water. It sounded like the restroom was empty. Then I pushed the door open and went in.

The restroom was small, a curious mix of white square

tiles that spread out over the floor and crawled up the walls to about shoulder height and above that walls painted in more of that purple-red tint. Ceiling too. They must have gotten a discount.

There were four stalls and four urinals and four sinks and above the sinks the wall was one long mirror. There were stacks of rectangular paper towels on the shelf that ran below the mirror and behind the sinks. Water trickled from the stall closest to me as a leaking toilet cistern constantly refilled itself.

I did two things, the *second* of which was to go over to the last cubicle in the row of four and open the door and take a look at what was lying on the floor.

But the first thing I did was a surprise, even to myself. I watched myself in the mirror and I watched myself do it and I wondered all the time why I was doing it. Because the first thing I did was turn to face the first sink and look at myself in the mirror. And I told myself I was doing that because I had noticed that the top button of my coat had come undone again and I was just using the reflection to make sure I did it up right. The coat was extra large and the buttons were pretty big but I had fat fingers made of a magical steel and titanium alloy that federal scientists had spent five years and as many millions of dollars getting just right, and those fat fingers just hadn't done the button up properly earlier.

At least that's what I told myself.

I tugged at the button and I tugged at the buttonhole and I brought them toward a happy meeting. Afterward the coat felt tight.

I paused and looked at myself and in the mirror I saw a man in a wheelchair and I heard a lot of noise and then both things were gone.

Then I looked at myself and then I undid the top button and then all the rest and then I pulled the lapels of my coat apart. Underneath I was wearing a brown suit with yellow pinstripes and under that a cream shirt that had a nice weave to the cotton and a tie that was blue with a green stripe. I thought it all went rather well against my chassis, which was bronzed and the color of those sculptures by that guy who did sculptures in bronze.

I didn't know how I knew that. It was a memory. A nugget of knowledge wedged behind a bank of hot transistors. An echo of Professor Thornton, my creator, whose mind had been used as the template of my own. Maybe he liked bronze sculptures. Maybe he collected them.

This happened sometimes. Echoes. Flashes. Sometimes it was little things, like the smell of pipe smoke and the feel of wool against the back of my neck and that feeling you get when someone you don't know very well makes you a meal and you're not sure they are a good cook and then it turns out they aren't a good cook but a great cook and the meal is wonderful and you're happy and relieved and eager for another glass of wine.

Like I said. Little things.

Sometimes the echoes were not so little. Echoes like a man in a wheelchair and a lot of noise and the feeling of heat and the feeling that my trench coat should button up just fine but it didn't.

Echoes like that make me feel something. I don't know what that feeling is. I don't have a name for it. It's that feeling that's like paranoia but isn't. That feeling that there's something else going on in the world that you don't know about and you're not sure if everyone else is in on it or not or has the same feeling.

Maybe that is paranoia.

I looked in the mirror and that feeling came and went like a lapping tide and I remembered a fire and someone talking in a language I didn't know and someone talking with a voice that sounded like a chainsaw going through a stand of bamboo.

And then it was gone. The tape in my chest wound ever onward.

I blinked, or at least my optics did the mechanical equivalent, and I looked in the mirror and I realized I had not only unbuttoned my coat but my jacket and shirt too and I had pulled my tie to one side. I hoped that no-

body had to use the facilities, because walking in on a robot taking a look at his own chassis was bound to make
someone feel a little uncomfortable.

But that's what I was doing. Looking. I wasn't sure
what I was looking at. There was my chest. Metal. Thick
metal. Bulletproof, in fact. I was built for law enforce-
ment, so that was probably a good idea. There was a lot of
stuff going on underneath that shell that a bullet would
be no good for at all.

Most important was my memory tape. A high-density
reel-to-reel magnetic record. It wasn't my brain. That was
sitting snugly behind my optics. It wasn't my permanent
store. That was a set of silicon chips on which were
recorded *Webster's* unabridged, the traffic regulations of
California, the flags of the world, and the address of my
tailor. Among other things.

But the tapes were me because I was really just like
anybody else, the sum total of my experiences and mem-
ories. Most of these were back at the office, in the store-
room behind the locked door. Only the last day's worth
of me was sitting in my chest.

Something bugged me about that, so I did what I had
to do and I took a look. Just to be sure. I undid the
catch on the inside of my chest with a stray thought and
popped the hinge and then my fingers did the rest.

My chest swung open. The tape was there, behind the

door, the reel reflected on the left slowly feeding the reel reflected on the right. There was some other stuff there too. Lights that flashed. Some switches. The master data port I used to plug myself into Ada back at the office and beside that a larger port that was my power inlet, which I used to charge myself back at the office when the day was done.

The tape moved slowly and silently and a couple of lights flashed.

I closed the door in my chest. Then I looked at the door itself. It was the same alloy as the rest of me but different. It wasn't bronzed. It was still shiny silver.

If I didn't know any better I would have said it was new. It fitted snugly but it arched outward. Not by that much but enough to make my cotton shirt a tight fit, and by the time I'd buttoned the suit jacket up and then the trench coat over that, the top button of the coat was pulled tight. Not a lot. But just enough to draw the big button out of its home.

I didn't know if it was important. It probably wasn't. I did all the buttons up and I straightened my tie.

Then the echo flashed in front of my optics. The memory fragment of the fire, the movie theater, the someone in a wheelchair.

"Okay," I said to my reflection.

Okay. Maybe I'd been damaged and Ada had had me

repaired. Nothing wrong with that—quite the opposite. I looked at myself in the optics and let my optics focus on the scratch on my cheek. It wasn't deep. It curved down like a sickle. I liked it, in a way. It wasn't that noticeable but if you did notice it you might call it distinctive. I remembered something about the noblemen of Germany working real hard on getting a facial scar from fencing back in the old days. Classy.

I guess Thornton had read a history book sometime.

I made a note to ask Ada about it. If I remembered, which, given the amount of tape left on my reel, was perhaps unlikely. So as I turned from the mirror and surveyed the cubicles I pulled a small yellow legal pad from one coat pocket and a mechanical pencil from the other and as I walked toward the only cubicle that had a closed door I made a note to myself to ask Ada about the repair. I don't know why I wanted to know, but I did, so I didn't argue.

When I got to the cubicle with the closed door I stowed the pad and the pencil and then I pushed the cubicle door open. What I saw beyond the door made me stop thinking about my new chest panel and returned my attention to where it was supposed to be.

On Honey.

The man's body was lying on the floor of the cubicle. He was wearing a suit. He was lying on his back and he was shoved up against the bottom of the toilet so his chin was pressed against his chest and his arms were up and dangling and the best description for his legs was "akimbo." It didn't look very comfortable but I figured he didn't mind on account of the hole in the middle of his forehead and the fair amount of red liquid leaking out from behind him down the toilet pedestal. The hole in his head was small and I didn't need to check the caliber. I patted my inside coat pocket and felt the mouse gun Honey had ditched in the Dumpster.

I took a snap of the body. I didn't much feel like touching it. I didn't much feel like being caught standing over it either. If the club was filled with patrons of a criminal disposition and they found a strange robot standing over the body of one of their buddies I was fairly sure they wouldn't be too happy about it.

Being a hit man—hit *robot*—is an interesting business. It requires a certain level of what I like to call *not being caught*. There were ways to avoid that particular outcome and I liked to think I was pretty good at a few of them. I had several advantages in my favor. I didn't leave fingerprints, for a start.

But there was a strange thing about being a robot. Being the *last* robot. And that was that if people did see me, they filed themselves neatly into one of two groups: they were either pleased to see me, or they weren't.

Those who were pleased usually expressed that pleasure with smiles and folded arms. Admiration from a safe distance. Those who didn't like me just kept away. They grimaced and frowned and some even shuddered, and then they turned away, man, woman, and child. It was like it was a natural reaction. An instinct that could be inherited and could not be controlled by the conscious mind.

There was even a word for it: robophobia. Ultimately it was robophobia that got the federal robot program cancelled, my permanent memory store told me. Some people liked robots but *most* people didn't. And *most* people were voters and voters are a slice of the population that people in power like to keep happy.

So the robots came and the robots went and the world kept on turning.

But the last robot in the world getting caught standing over the body of a gangster in the restroom of a famous club on Sunset Strip was just going to make my job a whole lot harder than it was already and I hadn't even killed the guy.

No. Honey had.

So I left and I left quickly.

I had a call to make.

5

Someone else was using the phone. The man had taken his hat off and had ducked under the green plastic dome and as he spoke he looked around like a deep-sea diver on a great underwater adventure.

I parked myself by the coat check and pulled down the corner of my hat. The coat-check girl was back and hard at work with her ifle. The man on the phone glanced at me, but then he turned his back and he kept talking.

I turned my audio receptors up and I heard the man say the following sequence of words into the mouthpiece of the telephone:

"Yes."

"No."

"Yes."

"Yes."

"Yes."

"Okay."

"You're sure?"

"Okay."

"Okay."

I assumed there was a voice on the other end of the line but I couldn't hear it. I tried to, but when I turned my audio receptors up all I got was the scratch of the coat-check girl's nail file.

Then the man in the green dome nodded and hung up. He had turned back around to face me and he stood there for a moment, staring at me through the misty green. Then he ducked out of the dome and without taking his eyes off me he put his hat on and he pulled it down over his forehead. It looked a little small and he tugged it twice but it just stayed floating where it was. Hat like that was bound to give him a headache.

He walked over to me and he leaned on the other end of the coat-check counter. The girl stopped filing her nails and looked at him and he gave her a look that I would have called lewd. Her only reaction was to bend her head back to the task at hand. Then the man sniffed and he nodded at the top of the girl's head but it was clear he was talking to me.

"Saw you before," he said.

I frowned on the inside. When I didn't answer the man glanced up at me from beneath the brim of his hat and that same brim dipped as he gave me a nod as tight as his hatband.

"You from out East?"

I didn't say anything. I wasn't from out East but I

didn't quite want to tell him that.

The man nodded toward the telephone. "Heard you talking earlier. Thought you might be from Tieri's mob."

He'd heard me talking. That was careless of me. Of course, I should have realized—the men assembled in the club might have been watching the dancers but they were also watching each other. Listening to each other.

And that included me because in the dark I was easy to mistake for one of their number. So he had heard me on the telephone, which meant he had heard my accent. Perfect, artificially programmed Brooklyn. Or so I've been told. I've never been east of the Sierras. Or so I've been told.

But I said, "That I am, pal," in a quiet voice while I contemplated the fact that a man named Tieri from New York had gone to the trouble of sending someone out to a club in Hollywood on a weeknight. I needed to talk to Ada to see if she'd found out more about the kind of business that was going on here and this guy in the too-small hat was currently stopping me from doing just that.

"Figured," said the man. He returned his attention to the top of the coat-check girl's head and he cocked his own as he watched her work on her nails. "I hope you brought a good deal of dough with you. Word is it'll go north of a cool million."

The man made a sound with his tongue behind his

teeth that wasn't a bad imitation of a small caliber round exiting the barrel of a mouse gun like the one I'd liberated from the Dumpster. I guess he'd heard a few of those in his time.

I glanced over to the front door of the club and I wondered if Honey had come back in yet.

I looked back at the man and I made a similar kind of sound. What I actually did was play him back a recording of himself, the pitch lowered just a hair.

The man liked this. He nodded. Then he seemed to change his mind and he shook his head. "Falzarano, am I right?" He shook his head again. "It's always like this when he's around. I mean, where does he get it from, eh? It's like he's a gangster or something."

I said nothing. The man looked at me. Then he laughed and he reached forward and he slapped me on the arm. Then he withdrew the hand and shook it a little like my arm had been a little harder than he expected.

"Hey, pal, I like you. I like you a lot. Tell Tieri I said hello. He's a great guy, great guy. Hey, I'll come see him soon. You tell Tieri that. Tell him to break out the Chianti, huh? Huh?"

Then he spun on his heel and he headed back toward the big double doors. "I'll see you in there," he said without turning around. And then the doors swung and he was gone.

I stayed where I was next to the coat check. I didn't have lips but I pretended to purse them like I'd seen people do on television. Or maybe it was Thornton who had watched TV. Whatever the case, it seemed to help with the process of thinking.

Then I walked over to the telephone booth. When I got there I lifted the receiver off the cradle and then I turned around to the coat-check girl. She was still leaning on her counter but now the file was still and she was looking at me.

"We're out of milk," she said. "And motor oil." She smiled.

"Cute," I said, and then I put the telephone back on the cradle. I put both hands in the pockets of my coat and then I used an elbow to point toward the club doors. "You know who that guy was?"

The coat-check girl shrugged. "Never seen him."

More of that lip pursing went on behind the flat immobile metal plates that made up my face. I liked the feeling so I kept doing it.

"Don't tell me, you never seen any of the others before either, right?"

The girl straightened up and she smiled. "A girl has to earn a living somehow," she said. "I'm hardly mining gold here."

She had a point. I nodded at her and she smiled again.

Then she nodded. We seemed to have reached an understanding and she turned and disappeared.

I pulled the telephone back to the side of my head and I dialed the number that was soldered into my permanent store. The line rang, then clicked, then went dead. That was how it worked. Contact had been established and nobody could break in on the line for a listen. Ada and I spoke to each other via an encoded signal. Not even the FBI could hear what we said.

"I think I need a TV for the office," said Ada.

"Uh-huh."

"Y'know," she said, "what with you out most nights, a girl gets lonely. And a TV is less work than knitting. Or petting a cat."

I glanced over a shoulder and aimed an audio receptor at the doors that led to the dance floor. Just then the kick drum was kicked and a symbol crashed and the Hit List were back on the stage.

I turned back around. "Did you get the pictures?" I asked.

I heard a tinkle that was the unmistakable sound of someone stirring a cup of coffee with a spoon and then there was a clatter like that spoon had been put down on a hard dull surface. I made a note to check the desk in the office for stains.

"I got them," said Ada, "but you're not going to win

the Pulitzer. The composition is lousy and you can forget about the lighting, believe me."

"Thanks for the critique. Did you make any of them?"

Ada laughed. It was light and airy like someone laughing at a dinner party before crushing the olive from their dry martini between two molars.

"You were right," she said. "A finer bunch of no-good hoods you will hardly find in the greater Los Angeles area. In fact, you wouldn't find any at all, as they all seem to be at the club."

"So I was right? They're villains?"

"I can name six out of seven."

"Care to share?"

"It's not the individual names that are of interest," she said. "It's who they represent."

"Don't tell me," I said. "One of those they represent is a guy called Tieri who operates out of New York City."

"Sounds like I didn't quite wipe all of the detective programming from your memory banks. I'm going to have to do some more tinkering. Tieri is a big name out east. Where did you hear about him?"

"I met a guy."

"Tell me about it."

"Here, at the club. He thinks I'm from Tieri's mob."

"Now, that's fairly interesting," said Ada. "Is he in one of the snaps you sent?"

"I think so. Who else did you pick?"

I could have sworn I heard the sound of sliding papers. Heavy papers. Photographic paper. Like there was someone in my office right now playing solitaire at the desk with my pictures.

"Well, now, we've got two boys who work for a guy called Malone. We've got two more boys who work for a guy called Pavone."

"Four men representing two gangs. Okay."

"There are three more pictures. One of them I think is a guy called Aspen. Word was he worked for a guy who worked for a guy called Boxer, but that info is out of date."

The band was still playing in the other room. I watched the door and pressed the telephone to my metal cranium.

"Where did you get all this from, anyway?" I asked.

"I'm going to assume that's a rhetorical question, Ray. Because a girl doesn't reveal her sources."

"I thought that was newspaper men?"

"I forget," said Ada. "Truth is the information is a little patchy on this. My data banks could use an update."

"Remind me next Christmas."

"I may just do that," said Ada. "Anyway, the only other one I can identify is a guy who works for Zeus Falzarano. Now, there's a piece of work."

A circuit lit up somewhere inside me. "Falzarano. He came up in conversation. Something to do with a million bucks in cash."

"Hold on there, Ray, I'm going to need to sit down. A *million* bucks?"

"Apparently so. My new friend said he hoped I'd brought a lot of dough, because it could go as high as a million bucks if Falzarano was involved."

"Oh, Raymondo," said Ada. She was positively cooing. "I could use a million bucks."

I should have known better to start talking to Ada about money. She was a computer that was programmed to run a profit. That was why she'd tweaked my master protocols in the first place, turning me from a second-rate private eye to a first-rate killer for hire. Turns out squeezing people until they stopped breathing was quite the earner.

"It's a sale," I said. "Has to be. Everyone is here to buy something. Something that could go as high as a million bucks."

"To buy," said Ada, "or to *bid*."

"Right," I said. That made a lot of sense. "An auction. They're all here for an auction, on the same night that we get a contract to take out a go-go dancer at a club that's being used as the auction venue."

"Sounds like a world of trouble, chief."

I paused a moment. Ada must have felt it in her circuits.

"Now what?"

"The pictures," I said. "Anyone there from Tieri's mob?"

"That's a negative."

"I thought there was one picture you couldn't hang a name on?"

"There is and not yet. But if that guy was from Tieri's mob I would have expected the name to pop like the rest."

"Unless he's hired someone new whose photograph hasn't landed on some law enforcer's desk yet."

"You could be right. Like I said, I might be a little behind the times. But I'll keep working on it."

I nodded to myself. Then I thought of something else.

I said, "Oh."

"I don't like the sound of that *oh,* Ray."

I checked that there was nobody around me. There wasn't. The band played on.

"I think I know where Tieri's man is."

"Okay."

"He's in the bathroom."

"Nature's call, Ray, nature's call. Am I going to have to teach you about human biology now?"

"I know enough about human biology to know that

they tend to leak red stuff when they get punctured."

"Oh," said Ada. "He's not coming out of the bathroom, is he, Ray?"

"He is not."

"How did you do it?"

"I didn't."

"Okay. That place is full of creeps and they're all after something expensive. Someone loses patience and decides to take out a bit of the competition. I can see how that works."

"True enough," I said, "but that's not what happened."

"Okay, so who killed Mr. Unlucky from NYC?"

"Honey did."

"Very funny."

"I heard the shot and saw her stash the weapon." I patted my coat. "I've got it on me."

"Less funny."

"We know who she is?"

Ada made a sound like an old woman clacking her tongue. "We know her name and her location and the sad fact that she needs to stop breathing sometime before dawn. That's all we need to know. No dice on anything else."

I shorted my vocal unit to make a humming sound.

Ada sighed. "You want my advice, Ray?"

"I'm all ears, Ada."

"My advice is that you need to get in and do the job and then get out. The grand charity auction of the Blackhearted Pooh-bahs isn't any of our business, nor the murderous habits of a rogue go-go dancer. What is our business is making sure she doesn't get out of that building alive. You know where she is?"

There was a sound behind me. I looked around.

"I have a feeling," I said.

The front door of the club had opened. I saw a little of the street outside. Sunset Boulevard was busy. The lights on the corner were green. Cars cruised by in both directions.

Then the door closed and the girl who had come in stopped and looked at me. Tasseled red two-piece and high white boots and an expression on her face somewhere between a frown and a pout. Her eyes moved over me but that was all of her that moved. She stood as still as I did.

"I'll call you back," I said into the telephone, and then I hung the telephone up. I thought I heard Ada say "Good luck," but I wasn't sure and the receiver was already back on its cradle when Honey walked right up to me.

We were alone in the lobby. The coat-check girl hadn't rematerialized and the last time the big double doors had swung was when my new friend had disappeared back inside the club to catch the Hit List's second act.

I glanced over Honey's shoulder. The restrooms were behind her. There was already one body in there. Now it seemed like I had the chance to stash another. And why not? It was as good a place as any. There were other restrooms in the place. All I had to do was find an "out of order" sign and hang it up and Tieri's man and the mystery girl could rest in peace. At least until the cleaners came in.

I reached for the girl and she didn't flinch. In fact as I moved my arm she took another step forward and then she leaned in to my chest. She was at least a foot and a half shorter than I was and she had to look almost straight up.

I looked down at her. Her eyes were green.

"Let's talk," she said and she said it in a voice that was not afraid and was not trying to keep anything in particular quiet.

Then she stood back and she looked at the arm I still had outstretched. I'd been planning on taking a hold of her neck, but now she was standing too close. I felt a little silly with my arm out like that so I let it drop.

She jerked her head toward the restroom door and she went over and disappeared through it.

She sure was making it easy for me.

But as I crossed the lobby I decided that I'd ask her a couple of questions first.

Maybe Ada was right. Maybe I shouldn't be thinking like this, shouldn't be asking questions that had nothing to do with the job.

Maybe Ada was right and she should take a look at my programming, make some more adjustments, expunge this streak of curiosity that seemed to have appeared among the transistors and neuristors inside my head.

But as I pushed open the restroom door I wasn't sure I wanted Ada to do anything of the kind.

6

Honey was leaning against one of the basins. She had her arms folded over her bare midriff and she was looking at the fourth cubicle along. I'd closed the door behind me when I'd taken a look earlier but now there was a large circle of blood pooling out from under it.

I stood next to Honey and I didn't say anything. She nodded at the door.

"That was unfortunate, but necessary," she said. The echo off the white tiles made her voice sound deeper than it had out in the lobby. I put her accent somewhere in Eastern Standard Time.

Then she nodded again, but this time it was toward the back of the restroom, beyond which was, by my guess, the parking lot. "I dumped the piece. They'll find it easy enough once they find Bob here, but we'll be clear by then."

"If you say so," I said. When I spoke, Honey turned and looked up at me and her lip curled at the edge. Her eyes went up and down then resettled on my optics. The lip curled some more. Whatever she was looking for, she seemed to like it.

"I'm glad they sent you. Things could get a little heavy."

I considered this. Sure, things were going to get a little heavy, but not in the way she was thinking.

But there was another surprise.

She'd been expecting me.

The thought buzzed around my voltage control stack like an angry wasp. It sure was a doozy. Not only had she been expecting help, but it was no surprise that they'd sent a robot. Even though I was the last of them left walking.

I wondered whether I should point that out to her.

Instead I took a step toward the cubicle, keeping out of the blood. The grout that held the white tiles to the floor was also white and it was staining badly. The janitor was going to throw a fit.

"So who's Bob?" I asked. I took a bet. "One of Tieri's?"

Honey nodded. She moved to my side and peered into the cubicle. "Tieri's right hand. I met him last year in New York. I knew there was a fair chance he or one of the others would be here, but I was counting on him not recognizing me with this get up."

I looked at her. She held her arms out, indicating the two-piece and boots. I noticed that her shiny black hair was a wig.

"I didn't know you'd been out to New York," I said, which was the truth and nothing but. Honey glanced back at the dearly departed Bob, but she nodded in response.

"Boxer was putting feelers out," she said, "trying to get Tieri onside. You know, after the recent troubles. We've got a lot of rebuilding to do. But Tieri was being difficult so of course Boxer sent his girl out, to try to smooth things over. Didn't go over too well." Honey grimaced at the memory. Then she looked at me. "But you know Boxer. When he gets an idea, wild horses can't stop him."

I nodded and as I nodded I wondered how out of date Ada's information on the gangs of Los Angeles was. She'd mentioned this guy Boxer and it didn't take a private detective to understand that Honey was Boxer's "girl" and on his payroll. And she thought that I was too.

I was starting to get a better grip on the events of the evening. I'd walked into the middle of a mob auction for a mysterious something worth a million bucks. Gangsters from all over town and beyond were here to bid, putting aside grievances and territorial disagreements just for one night.

Except for Boxer. He'd sent Honey here, and Honey was not only in disguise but had taken out Bob from Tieri's outfit for fear he would recognize her from New York.

Which meant Boxer was not playing by the rules. If his kingdom was crumbling, his alliances—including a potential one with Tieri—failing, then he might be short of funds. And if he was short of funds, then he couldn't afford to bid at the auction for a mysterious something worth a million bucks.

But it was something he still wanted. Wanted enough to send someone in to get it, by any means that did not involve money.

I looked down at Bob's body. His face was white and getting whiter as the blood trickled out of him about as fast as the water trickling out of the leaking toilet cistern.

Honey was not only an assassin. She was a thief. She was here to steal the mysterious something.

"Wild horses," I said, and maybe I said it to myself. Honey just looked at me but the frown on her face didn't stick around very long. I pointed at the body. "Shame about Bob," I said.

Honey dropped her arms. "Didn't leave me much choice. Boxer's playing his last card on this one." She nodded at the body. "I picked a piece from one of the Malone mob and used that. He'll find it missing before the night is out. Chances are he'll notice it's gone before they find Bob here, and then when they start looking they'll find Bob and then the gun and the spotlight goes onto Malone. By then we'll be fifty miles away with the package. They'll be too busy fighting among themselves to even think of coming after us or Boxer."

"Neat plan," I said. Then I thought about my new friend in the too-small hat. "I think I might have bought us some more time, too. One of the buyers out there thinks I'm from Tieri's mob—they think I'm Bob. So maybe they won't be looking so hard if they see me around."

Honey's eyes went wide. She had pink makeup around them and the pink got paler as her skin stretched. Underneath those wide eyes was a big smile.

"Even better," she said. "They'll be expecting Tieri's lug to be at the auction and now they think that's you. That's good. That's *very* good."

I nodded like I meant it, and I had to admit I did. She made a good point. Anything that made my job—my *real* job—easier tonight was no bad thing.

"Okay," I said. "How do we get the package?"

Honey turned away from Bob's cooling body. She walked back to the sinks. She stopped and looked at me in the mirror. She said, "How much did Boxer tell you?"

"Not much," I said. "Nothing, in fact."

This was true given that I had never met him.

Honey pursed her lips. Seemed like she was considering something. She still had her arms folded. She turned her head to look at the door.

"Okay, I can fill you in," she said. "Fix the door. We don't have much time. The auction starts at midnight."

I looked at the door, then I walked over to it. Hanging

on the back was a small sign on a piece of string. It was turned over to show the blank side. I turned it around. The sign said OUT OF ORDER. I flicked it off the hook, opened the door, and hung the sign the right way around on the outside.

I checked my internal chronometer. It was eleven thirty. A half hour to the auction.

Then I turned back to Honey. I looked at her. She was leaning one hip against the sink. Her arms were folded. She seemed pretty relaxed. I guessed that she was used to this kind of thing.

Then I thought about finishing my job here and now and getting out, like Ada had said. All of this business was none of mine. I needed to be somewhere else. I needed to avoid getting involved.

I considered the target. I estimated maybe forty seconds to put Honey's lights out in a permanent way. Make it a round sixty. No point hurrying. Stash the body. Give me another minute as I'd have to tread carefully to keep out of Bob's blood. Then I could leave and there would still be twenty-eight minutes before the auction started and Bob was missed. Malone's boy might have patted his pocket for his gun before then, but it still felt like I had a comfortable cushion.

The job that had looked difficult suddenly looked a lot easier.

And then Honey asked, "How long have you been with Boxer?"

"Not long," I said. I said it without hesitation because I was still telling the truth and the truth tends not to take too long.

She nodded. She smiled. She lifted her head. "Good thinking of him," she said. "Even if it cleaned him out."

I said nothing. She lifted her head a little higher. "Hiring a robot. The *last* robot. I wondered where all his money went. But you seem like a good investment."

I still said nothing, but I gave a small shrug that was, frankly, rather noncommittal, and hoped Honey would change the subject.

"You ever run into Falzarano's gang?" she asked. As I considered her question I felt a circuit board inside me start to cool down nicely.

"Falzarano," I said. "I know the name, but not much more than that."

"He was the kingpin of LA," she said. "Ran every racket going. Some people even say he ran the city itself. Those people might not be wrong either."

That chimed with Ada's comment about Falzarano being a piece of work. "Was?"

Honey shrugged. "He went into retirement. He's old now. He's got a mansion up in the hills—big place, fortified like a castle. We don't think he's stepped out of the front door in years."

We. Her and Boxer.

"Okay," I said. "So tell me about the auction."

Honey licked her lips. "We heard about it weeks ago, something being organized, a meeting. Then two weeks ago Boxer got me to fold someone from Bay City back into the water, and I found an invitation in his jacket. Turns out every outfit in town had got them—everyone except Boxer, of course. I felt around for more information, got word that it wasn't just LA—the auction was *national*. People were coming in from all over just for this."

I nodded. "People like Bob from New York."

"Oh, and a lot more than that," said Honey. "Reps from just about all of the lower forty-eight are here."

Twenty minutes to midnight. I wished I'd taken more photographs for Ada to ID.

"And with everyone under one roof, and without an invite, Boxer just sent you in?"

Honey smiled. "Well, I am the best he has. And anyway, he didn't just send me, did he? He sent you as well. He didn't tell me because he must have figured the less each of us knew, the less likely we'd accidentally tip the others off."

"Ah, right," I said. "But I still don't like the odds."

"Things go the way we've planned, the odds are very much in our favor."

I paused. I narrowed my optics at her but I'm not sure she noticed. There was one thing that still bugged me.

The package. The mysterious something worth a million bucks that Honey here was going to somehow steal from out under the noses of every gang from the Pacific to the Atlantic.

I still didn't know what it was.

So I asked her, and this time it was Honey's eyes that narrowed. "Boxer didn't tell you much, did he?"

"Boxer was pretty busy," I said.

Honey paused.

"Okay, so the package," I asked, "how are you going to get it and get out of here with all of your limbs still connected?"

Bob's blood was nearly lapping at my loafers.

"What's the time?" asked Honey.

I checked. "Eleven forty-two, PM."

"We're out of time. I need to get in there. Just come in with the others and keep your eyes open. And be ready to leave in a hurry."

I needed more information than that. I had a lot of questions forming and I wanted Honey to answer them. But I just stood there and she left the restroom. I watched the door swing behind her and then I looked at myself in the mirror. The top button of my coat had popped again. I squeezed it home.

Then I went out of the restroom and into the lobby. The coat-check girl was back. The band had stopped playing. I could hear the traffic cruising along Sunset Boulevard just outside the main doors on my left. I couldn't see Honey anywhere.

Fifteen minutes to go.

I walked over to the big double doors and stepped back into the club.

7

The club had entered a lull. The crowd looked thinner, and those who were left were quietly enjoying their cigarettes and alcohol. The air was full of smoke that hung almost motionless, a fug indistinct but ever present. It was like looking at the world through dirty dishwater.

The hoods had gone, all of them, their absence creating a not insubstantial amount of free space at the bar, which was itself now unattended while the stage at the far end of the room was occupied by the musical instrumentation of the Hit List but not by the Hit List themselves. One guitar leaned against the rim of the big bass drum. Another guitar lay on the floor. The amps behind them hummed. I listened. Fifty-nine point nine five hertz. Same as the wall socket they were plugged into.

The dance floor was deserted and the birds had flown from gilded cages that hung above it.

I wondered if the other three birds knew that one of their number was an imposter. An imposter that had given them a run for their money up there in the air, it had to be said.

I walked in and the double doors sucked shut behind me and something moved in the fog to my right. I glanced over and saw a man in a white shirt leaning with his elbows on a small round table, his neck craned around to watch me. It was the boyfriend. He had a cigarette in one hand and an expression that could only come from sucking a lemon or, as I glanced around to check, being abandoned by his girl.

Then the expression changed and he smiled. His eyes were only half open and one elbow slid a little on the bar. Any sudden movement and I was going to be picking him up off the floor.

"Drinks are on the house," he said. He raised his other hand to show me the tumbler he was holding. It was made of cut glass and it was filled with an amber liquid. He gestured with the glass toward the bar. "They told me I could have anything I like and not to worry about the check." He chuckled to himself. "They said any friend of the family was a friend of theirs too."

Then he drained his glass and he sat it on the table with a fair amount of force.

"What family?" I said. I looked around. His girlfriend had left with the others because—

Because she *was* one of the others.

I turned back to the boyfriend. "What's your girl's surname?" I wondered if the answer would be *Falzarano*.

"Nuts to ya," he said. "I know what to say and what not to say so go boil your head."

He sniffed and looked away. He lifted his empty glass and took a sip of nothing. He pulled the glass away from his mouth like it was hot and scowled at it like it had just insulted his mother. Free booze courtesy of his girl-friend's mob pals didn't seem to be doing much for his demeanor. I couldn't blame him. Not much of a life being the trophy on her arm. I imagined she took him to lots of funny places and told him to be good and to not talk to strangers.

I pulled my hat down low over my eyes. He saw me do it. Then he pointed a limp wrist in another direction. I looked over and saw there was a door by the side of the bar.

"They're all in there," said the man. "All of them. And her. Powdering her nose, right? Right."

He made a noise that was less like a laugh and more like the sound a man makes when he regrets the hole he has found himself in. "That damned band wasn't even any good. Grow your hair long and talk like the Queen of England and everybody around here loves you. Philistines."

"That's a big word," I said. The man screwed his eyes tight and then opened them again. He looked at me with a frown, like he hadn't seen me there before. He was swaying on his chair like a sea captain in a rough sea. Heading straight for the iceberg.

And then the telephone rang. Not the one out in the lobby. The one behind the bar. The guy at the table seemed to wake up a little, but now he was frowning at the ceiling.

I had a feeling I knew who was calling and who they wanted to speak to so I walked over to the bar and then I walked behind it. Some people watched me. Some didn't.

The telephone was on a shelf near the register. It kept ringing and as it rang I looked at myself in the mirror behind the bar. I could also see the reflection of the guy at the table. He was frowning at his empty glass.

I picked up the telephone.

"Hello, Ada," I said into the receiver. I kept my eyes on the guy at the table. Then I glanced to my left. The shelves behind the bar were filled with lots of bottles filled with lots of liquids.

"Everything okay, chief?" said Ada.

"This is third conversation we've had in one evening," I said. "I may not remember how things usually go down, but I'm starting to wonder if this is some kind of record."

My optics fell onto a bottle near the top that looked nice. I reached up and pulled it down. I couldn't drink it but the guy at the table could. He looked like he could use cheering up.

"A girl gets worried, Raymondo. Especially a girl with money riding on the outcome."

"Of course," I said.

"I don't like difficult any more than you do," she said, and when she said it there was an edge to the voice in my head. It was still Ada and there was still the creak at the back of her voice and when she spoke I still had the image of an older woman with hair that was too big and lines on her face that were kind. But there was something else there now. It was harder. More metallic. Like she was pressing the phone tight against her jaw and squeezing the mouthpiece with a hand that was too tight.

But Ada wasn't a person. She was a computer, one the size of an office.

I decided to follow the example of the guy at the table and I did my best to frown into the telephone's mouthpiece. I had a feeling I succeeded.

"Of course," I said. "But listen, time is ticking. The auction is due to start in just a few minutes. But I had an interesting conversation with Honey."

"I'm listening."

"She's here for the package too," I said. "She works for this guy Boxer."

"Huh," said Ada. "Well, I did say I was out of date. But listen, you can fill me in *after* you've done the job. It'll make an excellent epilogue to the paperback edition. In the meantime, who she works for doesn't matter half a dime to the likes of you and me."

"Okay," I said.

There was a pause on the line. Ada was still there. The line was dirty, a side effect of the way we used it, communicating via the coded pulse signal so nobody could listen in, but somewhere buried in the crackle was the ticking of the second hand of a stopwatch. I could imagine the big tapes back in the computer room spinning one way then the other and the lights underneath flashing an angry sequence.

Ada was thinking things over. I wasn't sure I liked it when she did that.

I sighed. "Is something wrong, Ada?"

"You tell me, Ray."

"Tell you what, exactly?"

Now it was Ada's turn to sigh. "You *are* going to get the job done, right?"

I made a sound that was a good impression of the gears in my Buick slipping on a cold morning.

"That wasn't the answer I was looking for," said Ada.

"I'll get the job done," I said. "That's what I'm programmed to do, right?"

"Right."

I hung the telephone up. I stayed where I was behind the bar for a couple of minutes. Midnight approached.

The auction. The guy at the table had slumped down and his eyes were closed. The cigarette was still burning between his fingers. Around him people drank and checked their watches and looked forlornly over at the empty stage.

I thought about Honey. I thought about the mysterious something. I thought about the other something in Ada's voice.

She was worried. And if she was worried then there had to be a good reason. And if there was a good reason then I wasn't going to waste any time arguing.

I had a job to do and I was running out of time to do it. Whoever it was that Honey worked for, whatever she was going to do with the mysterious something, it was not my business. I told myself that a few times and I also told myself that I didn't care either.

I turned around. I grabbed the bottle I'd picked from the top shelf. I read the label. I looked up into the mirror. The guy was still asleep.

I walked over to him. He didn't move. I put the bottle down with a thump and he moved now, his head jerking around at the sound. He looked at the bottle and then he looked at me and then he yelped as the cigarette burned down to his fingers.

"Party for one," I said. The man shook his burned hand and he looked up at me with a scowl.

Nice guy.

My clock struck midnight.

I left him to it and headed to the auction room.

8

The doorway led to a corridor, which led to another door which led to a corridor. More doors here. The floor was tacky underfoot. At first I thought I was tracking Bob's blood all the way from the men's room but then I saw it was just a dirty floor.

There were sounds coming from the door to my right. I stopped where I was and listened closely. This was the room. Then I took off my hat and then put it back on my head. I pulled it down as far as it would go and then I slipped it off the back of my head so I could pull it down some more. Then I lifted the collar of my trench coat and spent a few seconds working on the folds of the fabric so the collar would stick up nicely. It made me feel a little better.

I reached for the doorknob and I turned it and opened the door and passed myself through a crack as small as I could manage. Then I closed the door like nothing had happened.

The room was square. Like the other one I'd found, this one had stacks of chairs along two sides but some of those chairs were unstacked and had been set out in four rows in the middle of the room. On these chairs sat the men from the club. Three dozen total. Most kept their hats on. Some didn't. Some sat together. Some didn't. Some sat silently. Some murmured to each other. Some draped their arms over the back of the empty chair next to them and tried to look as easy as possible while they sized up the competition around them.

Only two guys in the room looked around from their chairs as I came in. One of them did nothing but turn back around. The other one gave me a nod that was as small as the first sip of too-hot coffee. Then he turned back around too. It was my friend with the too-small hat.

There were empty chairs, but I didn't want to draw any more attention to myself so I kept at the back and I sank against the wall by the door where the shadows were deep. Hoods seemed to like dark rooms. If anyone else wanted to take a peek all they'd see was a hulk in a hat and coat just like all the other hulks in hats and coats in the room.

No problem.

I looked around the room. There was something in the air. A certain kind of tension. The hoods had agreed not to kill each other for one night and so far that truce was holding. Although whether the truce would remain in place once Bob's body was found in the toilet I didn't like to speculate.

But things were coming to a climax. This was what they were all here for.

The auction.

The something in the air was excitement.

I kept on looking around. I'd been wrong about the hoods. They weren't guarding the approaches while their bosses met in secret. Their bosses weren't here. The hoods were here for them. It made sense. All the bosses in one room was a bad idea. They wouldn't meet in a club. They'd meet in a bunker. Under a volcano. On a deserted island in the Indian Ocean. Somewhere a lot safer than West Hollywood. Although not, apparently, with their old pal Boxer.

So the bosses weren't here. There was also no sign of Honey and there was no sign of the other go-go dancers either. But there was one woman in the room. She was sitting in the second row right in the middle. She sat with a straight back and her knees together and her hands resting on her lap. I could only see the back of her head but that head was covered with blond hair that curled into a cloud around the edges.

The girlfriend.

I felt sorry for the boyfriend. Not that it was any of my business.

In front of all the chairs was a big table and behind the table were three empty chairs. There was nothing on the table but above it hung a lamp from the ceiling. There were other lamps dangling down on short cords but the one above the table was the only one that was on. For a spotlight it wasn't too bad, and it kept the rest of the room dark, which was how we all liked it.

I checked my clock. It had struck midnight and it was heading toward five minutes past. No sign of Honey. No sign of any auction starting. The murmuring continued. The girl in the second row was as still and as silent as I was.

Then a door opened. Not the one I had come through but a door a few yards away on my left, stacked chairs towering on either side. In walked three men. Two of them were tall and young and had dark hair that was slicked back and they both wore big black sunglasses.

The man in the middle was old enough to be their father. He had hair that was gray and thin on top. It was slicked back with something shiny just like the hair of the two boys. He had a long hooked nose and a chin that stood just as proud of his face. He was shorter than his pals and as wide as the two of them together. He had short arms and legs. He walked slowly. His suit was expensive and it enclosed his impressive girth with enough panache to make me want to send his tailor a bottle of scotch for Christmas.

The old man walked down to the front and then sat in the middle of the mostly empty front row and his two companions sat on either side of him but not before they both stood there waiting for their boss to plant himself first. While he did that they faced the crowd and they pointed their sunglasses around the place like a pair of new arrivals at an airport looking for their names on a card. Once their boss was seated he gave a huff and a nod. This seemed to be all the two boys needed to turn and sit and adjust their jackets. Their sunglasses stayed just where they were.

The arrival of the old man and his boys had an interesting effect on the room. It went quiet and still. It hadn't been loud before and nobody had been rolling their hips like the go-go dancers, but now any and all movement stopped. Murmurs stopped as breaths were held then slowly let out. Crossed legs that jiggled were stilled. Fingers tapping the backs of chairs halted. Nobody coughed and nobody cleared his throat but I was pretty sure a few Adam's apples bobbed up and down in a way I would be hard pressed to say wasn't nervous.

Nervous because of the old man. Maybe you'd go a step further. Say they were scared. And I knew why. It didn't take much detective work to put a mechanical finger on it. And the way a few of the hoods looked at each other while trying very hard not to move told me something else.

They were surprised. Which figured. The elderly party hadn't been out in the main club room earlier. In fact, word was he hadn't stepped out of his castle in the Hollywood Hills in years.

Zeus Falzarano.

This really was a special night. And if I were a hood from a rival syndicate then sure as hell I'd be holding my breath right now too.

Eight after midnight. Nothing was happening.

Nine after midnight. Something happened.

Another door opened. This one was at the back of the room, behind the big table. I checked the mercury-fluid links behind my optics a handful of times to make sure the electronic lenses were seeing what they told me they were seeing.

They were.

A girl came out first. She was holding a box. It was flattish, rectangular, made out of a dark reddish wood, like a jewelry box. It was twelve inches wide and a third that deep.

The girl was Honey and she held the box—the *package*—out from her body, like it was a reliquary containing the holy bones of the patron saint of criminal enterprise.

Behind her came the other three go-go dancers. Each of them held a gun in a delicate but firm grip. The guns weren't pointed anywhere in particular but the message their presence was designed to convey was fairly clear. The trio filed through the door then fanned out around the table so they had the room covered.

Honey walked to the front of the table and stopped in front of Falzarano. Then she turned and placed the box onto the table with a respectful delicacy. Then she turned back around and stood to one side so everyone in the room could get a view. She didn't look at Falzarano but she didn't look at me either. Her expression was flat and her gaze was on the back wall.

I assumed this was all part of her plan so I stayed where I was and kept as quiet and still as everyone else.

Under the light above the table the wood of the box shone even redder. I adjusted my optics and took some souvenir snaps as I admired the fine grain on the box's lid. No sooner was I done than the blond woman got up from the second row. A few of the hoods shifted in their seats as they took in the view.

There was an empty chair on either side of her. She turned to the right and moved past the empty chair and then she stopped at the next one along. The lug occupying the pew in question took a moment to get the message, but when he did he jerked to life, standing quickly and holding the flaps of his jacket together as the woman slid past him.

Like everyone else in the room I watched her. When she got around to the front I watched her some more. I took a picture. It was going to come out well, on account of the fact that like her boyfriend she was quite a sweetheart and right then she was smiling a smile bright enough to make a man jump off the O of the Hollywood sign.

Above the smile was something else entirely. A look. A something dark and cunning that lived behind her eyes. A look that told me all I needed to know.

Power. She had it. Whoever she was. In a room full of hoods, standing in front of Zeus Falzarano himself, she had power. She had power and she knew it.

She lifted a hand and she placed it on the box so gently she was hardly touching the thing at all.

The thing that was the source of her power. The box was hers.

She was the seller.

"Gentlemen," she said and she said it with her chin pointed down and with her eyes scanning the audience from beneath her brows. She could hold the attention of a man in a way that only his favorite sports team could and she knew that too.

Oh, she was good. Of that I had no doubt. I could see now she was older than I'd first thought, more than a few years separating her from her boy waiting out in the club.

And with those years came experience and a certain kind of confidence which was now proudly on display.

"Thank you all for coming," she continued, talking through her smile, her blond hair flashing in the light that hung alone above the table behind her. "I know what it took to bring you all here. I know a lot of you have come a very long way for this."

Her gaze dropped down to Falzarano and her smile flickered at the corners. She gave him a nod.

"Mr. Falzarano, it is truly an honor."

Falzarano gave a quiet laugh and muttered something that might have been Italian. Then he waved a hand at her, rolling it in the air, a gesture both acknowledging her greeting and telling her to get the hell on with it.

The woman interlaced her fingers in front of her lap and addressed the room.

"As you know, I invited you all here because I have recently acquired a unique item which I believe will be of great interest to you and your syndicates."

I looked at the box on the table. I wondered what was inside it and what could possibly be so important and so valuable. Diamonds? No. The woman had said *item*, singular. Not stones, but jewelry, then. A famous piece, recently stolen? I'd probably read about it in the paper, only I had no memory of it as I had no memory before breakfast this morning.

Whatever was in the box, it was enough to draw hoods from all over the country to the back room of this club in West Hollywood and it was enough to bring the reclusive Falzarano down from his castle. It was enough for Boxer to send his best—Honey—to come to steal it, switching herself in for one of the dancers so she could get in nice and close. Which, on the face of it, seemed like a pretty good plan. All she had to do next was get out of the room with it.

That particular requirement seemed like it would present more of a problem.

The blond woman turned the wattage of her smile up a notch. She unlinked her hands and moved one to float over the box while sending the other plunging down the front of her blouse. Her blouse was a black number with ruffles, and from within she pulled out a key on the end of a slim chain hanging around her neck—a key which, thus extracted, she slid into the lock on the front of the jewelry box before giving it a half turn counterclockwise. I half-remembered a saying about being able to hear a pin drop, but tonight the tiny click of the lock disengaging sounded as loud as a bank vault being unsealed.

The auctioneer picked the box up and turned it around, the open lid resting against her middle, as she presented the contents to the assembled. She gestured to the star attraction within with the sweep of an elegant hand.

I wouldn't have said what went around the room was a gasp. Men like that didn't gasp. What they did was clear their throats and sit up straight and shoot looks at each other and adjust their ties. Me, I did less gasping on account of the fact that I couldn't breathe as a matter of course. But what I did do was focus my optics on the object nestled on a velvet bed inside the box. It was small and dull and silver and I didn't know what I would do with it if it was mine, but I suddenly had a very great urge to find out what it was for.

"Gentlemen, I think you all know the secrets this can unlock, and what those secrets are worth to you."

With those words that urge just got a great deal stronger. So strong that I came to a decision.

The thing in the box had no intrinsic value. I could see that. But what it represented was clearly important, so important that there were people in this room who were prepared to pay a fortune for it and a girl who was prepared to kill so she could steal it.

And I was going to help her. Because, that thing in the box, I wanted to know all about it and I thought Ada might like a little look-see too.

I settled back and thought over what I was going to do next.

Kill the girl. Take the box.

My job just got a whole lot easier.

9

If the room had been quiet before, it now fell into a hush as deep as the deep green sea. It was so quiet all I could hear was the ticking of a clock. The fast hand of a stopwatch forever speeding into the future.

I wondered if I should call Ada, tell her about the new plan. But there wasn't time and I wasn't sure she would be too pleased, at least not until she saw what I was currently planning to bring back to the office.

So instead I stood just where I was and I kept my optics on the auctioneer and the box and the mysterious something on the velvet bed within.

The auctioneer paused, playing that smile over her audience like a spotlight searching for an escaped prisoner.

"Gentlemen, we open the bidding at one hundred thousand dollars."

There came a series of sighs and hisses from different areas of the room, like someone had let the air out of all the tires in a car sales yard at once. Some looks were exchanged and some heads shaken. Everyone here must have known the starting price would be high but perhaps not that high.

My friend from the lobby broke the ice with a twitch of the newspaper in his left hand. He looked calm. He'd told me that he thought the item could sell for a million bucks. He seemed more prepared than the rest of them.

The auctioneer nodded. "Do I hear one hundred and ten?"

The auction had begun.

The bids began clawing for altitude. I watched and listened. Soon enough the auction became a two-man race. Falzarano and my friend with the newspaper. The kingpin kept his bids running and my man kept his newspaper twitching like a dog's tail batting summer flies. Nobody else seemed that interested. They all watched and listened with the folded arms and stooped heads and bunched shoulders of defeat.

The price climbed. I didn't know who my friend with the newspaper represented. It wasn't Tieri, after all. Bob was growing cold in the toilet and sooner or later someone was going to ignore the OUT OF ORDER sign and Malone's boy would find his gun was gone. I cast an eye over the room but I had no idea who Malone's boy was. Could have been anyone. Could have been my friend with the newspaper.

"Four hundred thousand dollars," said the auctioneer. This was directed at the newspaper man. He didn't hesitate. His wrist twitched and the newspaper twitched with it and the price went up another rack.

Then it happened. Of course it was coming. It was all part of the show.

Falzarano raised a hand and he said, "One million dollars," in that heavily accented voice of his. I couldn't see the faces of his two boys but I could imagine their smiles.

The auctioneer gave Falzarano a little bow and then turned to the newspaper man. I thought that turn was a little pointed. She knew. Falzarano knew. The newspaper man knew it as well.

The paper moved again and this time it was more than a twitch.

The auctioneer looked at Falzarano. "One million, one hundred thousand."

The old man's head moved a little to the left and then a little to the right and then he gave a nod.

"One million, two hundred thousand," said the auctioneer.

My friend shook his head. The newspaper in his hand didn't move an inch. The auctioneer's smile shone down on the mob boss sitting in front of her.

"Sold to Mr. Falzarano for one million, two hundred thousand dollars," she said, and no sooner had she spoken than she snapped the lid of the jewelry box shut. She placed it down on the table behind her, then turned and began to applaud. She kept it going for more than a little while even though it was the only sound in the whole room.

Well now. One million dollars and change. A lot of change. Cool or hot, I'd be clapping too if I had just parked that in my lap.

Falzarano nodded. Then he leaned into his boy again. They whispered something. I turned my ears up but all I caught was in a language I didn't know how to process. Italian. But I thought I got the drift because the man gave a very curt nod and then he stood up very sharply, headed to the side door, and disappeared beyond it.

That was when Honey raised an eyebrow and did her level best to use it to point to the same door and the man who had just left.

I got the message.

While the rest of the room stood and began to form a line to kiss the ring of the retired kingpin to congratulate him on his purchase I slipped out the back without a sound.

10

Sunset Boulevard seemed about as busy at half past midnight as it was during rush hour. For a lot of folk the Hollywood night was young and the air was still good. I still wasn't breathing and the change in temperature didn't bother me but for some reason I felt better out of the stuffy back room of the club. So I pretended to take a breath that was both long and deep and then I picked up the pace and headed around the corner and into the parking lot. I could have gone out the back but I hadn't because I didn't want Falzarano's boy to know he was being followed.

There was a new car in the lot. It was parked horizontally to take up spaces designed for three cars. It was black. It was big but subtle. There was no acreage of hood and fins big enough to fly to the moon with. Instead it was long and shaped like a teardrop, everything tucked away, like a bird diving underwater. Classy. Expensive. Something European, not American. Something imported. Exotic.

Falzarano's ride.

I liked it.

I didn't know which of his two boys had driven it. Maybe they took turns. I even wanted to take the thing for spin myself. But one of them was currently up to his waist in the backseat, his ass presented in my direction as he leaned in to reach for something down in a footwell. When he was done reaching he stood tall. In one hand he held his sunglasses. In the other hand he held a briefcase. I took a good look. Black. Hand-tooled leather. Expensive. An import, like the car, like the two boys, like Falzarano himself.

The man closed the back door of the car and I had to appreciate the way the door swung on its hinges and the way it clicked into place with no effort at all and with the satisfyingly solid clunk of an old country manor being locked up for the night.

The man stopped where he was. He'd seen me. Which was fine because I was now standing right in front of him.

Then he grinned and then he dropped his sunglasses onto the ground and then he shoved the hand now free inside his jacket to reach for something I assumed had bullets in it. His hand stayed just where it was because before he got to his gun I had got to his wrist and broken all the bones therein.

The boy was good. He grimaced and his face went red and his eyes narrowed but he clenched his jaw so as not to make a sound. The boy was very good. He knew what to do. He knew he had to fight even with the odds so heavily stacked against him.

But the moment was fleeting and the fight went out of his eyes as I put my other hand around his neck and gently pushed him to the ground.

He didn't get up again.

I opened the back door of the car. I appreciated the engineering. It was all so precise. The door was weighted just so. As I pulled it toward me I knew every mechanical element of its construction had been designed and built by hand to be satisfying. You spent that much on a car, you wanted to be satisfied.

Then I picked the guy up and I threw him in the back and I admired the way the door gently drifted back to the closed position with a clunk that was neither heavy nor light but finely balanced in between.

The marvels of European engineering.

Then I picked up the briefcase. I felt the weight. I shook it a little by the handle and I admired the way the little stacks of bound cash inside gently shifted within.

Then I picked up the man's sunglasses. I put them in my pocket. I looked down. There was no sign of a struggle because there hadn't been one, and then I turned to look at the car. It was black and silent and the back windows were tinted and you couldn't see the body lying across the seat even from a foot away. Suited me just fine.

In the dull reflection of the car's rear window I saw the back door of the club fly open. I saw Honey run out at a fair pace. She was holding something in an old laundry bag. She had the bag pressed against her middle with both hands. Whatever was inside it looked rectangular, shallow, something like a good-sized jewelry box.

She stopped. She looked at the big black car and she looked at the briefcase in my hand. She nodded. She understood. Then she pointed her chin at a small blue Lincoln parked across the lot from my car.

"That yours?" she asked.

I pointed with the briefcase at the big Buick. "The other one."

Honey nodded again and headed straight for it. She didn't wait for me to follow. She got to my car and darted around it and opened the passenger door. She put the bag into the footwell. Then she stood up and looked at me across the roof.

"Let's go," she said. She got into the car.

I didn't need another invitation.

What had I said about this job getting easy?

11

I drove, but not too fast. Traffic was fair and we didn't need any undue attention.

Honey knew what I was doing because she kept quiet and she kept her eyes on the road as she sat next to me in the passenger seat. The bag was back on her lap and she had both arms wrapped around it. If anyone got a glimpse of us when we stopped at traffic lights they might have looked twice at the big guy filling out a trench coat who had kept his hat on and the small girl wearing not much, but this was Hollywood, California, and what people did in their cars was not anyone else's business.

She gave directions. A left, a right, a left again, and then straight. I knew the streets. I had a map of the city in my permanent store. I wasn't the kind of robot to get lost. I imagined the map had been essential for my old job. It sure was for the new one. I knew where to find people and I knew the best places to sneak up on them and I knew the best places to take them afterward. Although most often I left them where they were. That was a good trick, one of the tools I used to avoid suspicion. You kill someone and you move the body then that person's absence is noticed and when it is noticed people start looking and when people start looking they find things you don't want them to find. A body in a Dumpster in an alley will lead to things. I was good at not leaving fingerprints and at not leaving any other kinds of clues but even I wasn't perfect. Inviting people to look where I don't want them to look is asking for a world of trouble.

But you kill someone somewhere people expect them to be—in their office or in their kitchen or in a motel room in the arms of their mistress—and you make it look good then people are still suspicious but maybe they don't go looking quite so far as they should.

So goes the theory.

Except tonight I had my target sitting right next to me and I was driving her around. My plan had been to arrange an accident in the club, one involving my steel fingers and her windpipe. There was already one body in the joint along with a lot of men who, on the balance of probabilities, were probably not so keen on any undue attention. Nobody would have reported anything. In fact, they might well have helped cover it up.

That would have been a nice piece of work. Satisfying, in a professional sense. Like the weight of the door on Falzarano's crimemobile.

Now that was out the window, but things weren't all

bad. Honey was sitting next to me. So I couldn't kill her at work. But I could kill her somewhere else. Somewhere dark and quiet. She wouldn't be found for a while. I could make it look good. And then I'd be back in the office. Ada would be happy because I would have done the job and would have a briefcase full of miniature portraits of Grover Cleveland and William McKinley and, as a bonus, a jewelry box with something inside I thought she would really want to see.

I kept driving and I asked: "What happened back at the club? Last I saw you were in a roomful of people who were all carrying iron of some description and were probably not in a mood to be friendly."

Honey laughed. It made her tassels swing. She leaned an elbow up on her door and said, "I brought it in. I just took it out again."

I frowned on the inside. "You mean they just let you walk out with Falzarano's prize?"

Honey's only response was a shrug. This was a girl who had got a job done and knew she had done it well. I didn't blame her at all.

"Okay," I said, "So who was the auctioneer and where did she get it?"

Honey glanced sideways at me. An expression of some description flirted briefly with her face but I couldn't quite see what it was because I was too busy watching the road.

"Her name is Athena. I know a whole lot about her, if you consider *jack* to be a whole lot of anything. But Boxer knows her. Or knew her. They have a history, I think. I don't know and I don't want to know. But she's an independent operator. Doesn't work for nobody. I think Boxer's been on her tail for a while, ever since whatever good thing they had going went sour. But like I said, none of my business. What is my business is getting the package out of her hands and into mine."

"And into Boxer's," I said.

At this Honey just smiled.

"Huh," I said. "Athena," I said. I thought about it for a moment. "Suits her."

Honey laughed and the laugh pushed her chest toward the dash and pressed her head back against the headrest

"Suits her! Yeah, right, suits her!"

I eyed the telephone that sat on the cradle between her seat and mine. I thought Ada might like a little update on the situation and what I had in the car with me right now. Then I changed my mind and decided to make it all a nice surprise.

I still didn't know where the mysterious something came from and how Athena had got it or even what it was for. I took a left turn and pushed the car onward and I put those questions to Honey. All that got me was the same laugh, the same arched back, the same creak of leather as she pressed the back of her black wig into the seat behind her.

"You'd know as much about that as me, baby. But I can tell you what it's for, no problem."

She told me. As I listened I pursed my lips on the inside. It helped with my thinking and I liked it.

When she was done we sat in silence a while. Honey was smiling. I knew why she was smiling. If I had the box that was sitting in the footwell by the heels of her white leather boots then I'd be smiling too.

"So Athena," I said. Honey's smile stayed where it was while her eyes darted sideways in my direction. "Why was she selling it? Couldn't she have used it herself? Because it sounds to me like it's worth a whole lot more than that pocket change she sold it for."

Honey just shook her head. "That's not what she does. I told you, she's *independent*. She doesn't work for nobody anymore. That puts her in a particular kind of position. A dangerous one. So she specializes. She sells things. Guns, drugs, stones, people, information. Whatever she can get her hands on that she thinks a certain type might be interested in. Hell, she even sells *money*."

I nodded. "And what she was selling needs an organization to fully realize. Which she doesn't have."

"Which she doesn't *want* to have," said Honey. "Listen. She operates on the outside. What her customers do with their purchases isn't her business and she keeps it that way."

We drove on and I thought about Athena for a while. Then we took a left.

"How long have you known Boxer?" I asked. It seemed like a sensible question. We were, after all, two colleagues out on a job.

According to Honey.

Honey frowned again. "How long have I known Boxer?"

"Sure," I said. "You mentioned going to New York last year. You must have been working for him a while."

Honey turned to look at me with narrow eyes.

"You're asking how long I've known Boxer?"

I felt a resistor coil behind my faceplate grow warm. "Sure," I said.

Honey turned a bit more toward me. From the corner of my optics I could see the muscles cord in her neck.

"You said you worked from him," she said. "But you don't work for him, do you?"

I'd made a mistake somewhere.

"Because if you worked for him then you sure as hell would know who I was. He'd make sure of that."

I ran some audio back from earlier in the night. Honey had said she was Boxer's *girl*.

"And you'd sure as hell know that Boxer is my *father*."

Oh.

Then the telephone rang. I kept one hand on the wheel and I used the other to pick up the handset. Saved by the bell.

"I appreciate you keeping to the speed limit," said Ada inside my head, "but you're taking the scenic route back to the office."

I glanced at Honey. She was watching me but her whole body was tight, ready to run or to fight or most likely both. She dropped her hand onto the door handle, but we were going too fast for her to make a safe exit. I increased the pressure on the pedal under my foot anyway while I moved the hand holding the telephone to the wheel and the hand that had been holding the wheel to the button that was on the console on my side of the car, right by the door. There was a click that sounded from all around. It didn't have the velvety depth of the locks on Falzarano's car but mine were electric and the effect was much the same.

Honey was in the car with me and I wanted it to stay that way. I glanced at her and she didn't look too pleased, but so far she hadn't moved. She was still waiting for her moment.

I reversed the position of my hands and into the telephone I said, "What do you know about Boxer?"

"Sounds like your audio inputs need a retune, Raymondo," said Ada. "I told you, my information is out of date."

"What about a lady called Athena? Ring any bells?"

"Nothing there, Ray, nothing there. But questions make me nervous, Ray. You asking them makes me even more nervous. What's going on?"

I thought about that for a moment while Honey vibrated next to me and the roar of an ocean came down the phone line and into my head.

"Earth to Ray, come in Ray."

"Okay," I said.

"Okay what?" Ada asked. "Is the girl dead? She's not dead, is she?"

I looked sideways at Honey. Honey glared at me. She pushed her face forward just a little. Like she was trying to listen in on the conversation I was having with my boss. That wasn't going to happen. She could hear me speak but whatever Ada said in reply was beyond the capabilities of any part of the human ear to hear.

"I'm working on it," I said.

Ada sighed. There was no other sound. No coffee being drunk. No cigarettes being smoked. No creak of the office chair.

Not that there had ever been any of these sounds. Like a large part of my world, those only existed inside my head. Echoes. Fragments. Reminders of another life that wasn't mine to remember.

"Work on it a little harder, chief," said Ada. "You don't have much time left."

Ada was right but there was still some padding. "I have two hours," I said. Then I'd have no choice. I had to be back at the office and in my alcove. The memory tape inside my chest held only twenty-four hours of data and I'd burned through nearly twenty-two.

"Then use them, Ray."

I kept driving. The road was straight. We were heading west. Toward Bay City. Honey's eyes went to the windshield. We seemed to be on the right track for wherever it was she wanted to go.

"Ada," I said.

"Ray," said Ada.

"This information you don't have."

"You're becoming obsessed, Ray."

"I might be able to solve that problem for you."

Ada didn't answer straight away. What I heard in the second before she spoke sounded an awful lot like a cigarette lighter coming to life.

That was more like it.

"Tell me more, chief," said Ada.

"I'll fill you in at the office."

"Looking forward to it."

Then I hung up.

I kept on driving. Honey sat next to me and she was watching my hands as they eased the steering wheel.

She had to die. That was the job. I was a killer. I killed people. Ada got the jobs and I did the jobs and somewhere a numbered bank account got a little fatter. It didn't matter what the job was. The target could be the president of the United States or the president of the Midwest Carpet and Flooring Traveling Salesman Association.

It was what I was programmed to do.

And I had two hours left to do it. I kept on driving. I didn't speak and neither did Honey. Finally she seemed to relax a little bit, but it wasn't like before. She was still waiting, still ready.

"We're nearly here," she said. "Second right. Then kill the lights and pull into the lot. I don't think we were followed, but they might have taken a different route. And then you and I are going to have a particular kind of conversation."

I followed her directions and I killed the lights like she had asked and I rolled into the parking lot.

It was a motel. The kind where the parking lot was in the middle and the motel wrapped around it. Three levels with balconies. There was neon in the office window at the back of the parking lot but the neon was dead. The whole place was. There was a sign on the window of the office that said CLOSED UNTIL JANUARY. HAPPY NEW YEAR! but the year posted underneath wasn't this one or the next. The joint had been abandoned and was now slowly falling to pieces.

I picked a spot and nosed the Buick into it.

Honey turned to me.

"Now unlock my door and follow me. Room two ten. Second floor. Bring the case. There's a little something I have to take care of."

She slipped her prize out of the laundry bag and squeezed the door handle with her free hand.

I reached over and pressed the button on the console and four doors of the car unlocked themselves. Honey got out and didn't say a thing.

I got out and watched her as she walked across the parking lot with the box cradled against her bare middle. There were steel stairs that ran up to the balcony on the second floor and kept on going up to the third. She took the first exit. I watched her until she was out of sight and then I reached into the back of the car and got out the briefcase. That nice weight was still there.

Then I got out and I closed the driver's door. The hinge squeaked and the door felt light and disappointing.

At least that disappointment would be short-lived. In the morning I wouldn't remember Falzarano's car.

I gripped the briefcase and went up the stairs. They

were rusty and they shook and they rattled and they creaked. I didn't waste any time on them.

The balcony on the second floor gave a great view of the parking lot. I headed back the way I had come until I was standing more or less over my car. I checked the room numbers. Two ten was the next one over. The door was closed. The curtain was drawn tight and there was no light from within. The city had cut the utilities a long while ago.

I stood and I looked and I listened. There was nobody around to admire the great detective doing two things at once and there wasn't any sound from the room.

I reached for the handle. It was unlocked. I stepped inside. I closed the door. I looked around. It was dark and then suddenly it wasn't.

Honey was standing by a bed that was just a rotting mattress. The jewelry box was on the bed, as was the bound and gagged form of a lady wearing nothing but a set of matching underwear that covered not very much at all. She had black hair and she looked at me with eyes ringed with blue and pink makeup. She looked like she should be wearing the knee-high white leather boots and red two-piece covered in tassels that Honey was currently occupying.

The woman on the bed didn't move. Neither did Honey, on account of the gun pointing at her head along with the beam of a flashlight.

There were two other flashlights pointed at me along with four other guns.

Five of them. Two of us.

I recognized them.

The man holding the gun against Honey's head smiled. I tried smiling back but I'm not sure he saw it.

And then he said, "I'm so glad you could both make it," in an accent stiff enough to butter toast with.

He was English. Just like the other four men were.

The Hit List.

And I had a feeling I knew what they were going to ask for next.

12

"I would probably advise you to stand just where you are," said the Hit List's singer from underneath all that hair. I looked at his friends. There were in identical silvery suits and they all had the same volume of blond locks that had a tendency to drive ladies wild.

The Hit List. The only group at the club who hadn't been at the auction. I hadn't paid that any attention then and I knew that was my mistake now. Because it seemed they'd been there to sing for the same reason Honey had been there to dance. They were after the mysterious something the lovely Athena had been there to sell, just like everyone else in town.

Me now included.

I looked at Honey. She looked at me. She had both elbows locked and her arms straight by her side. There was only one gun on her and four on me but it wouldn't have taken much for one or more of those four guns to swing in her direction. I had a feeling the boys from across the pond knew what they were doing, the way they held their guns and their nerve at the same time. That was generally harder to pull off than it looked and they were doing a fine job.

Which meant they weren't a band. They were a gang, just like all the others that had turned up at the club for the auction. Only they'd come a little farther than the rest of them.

Honey looked at me and she said, "I'm sorry, Ray."

I glanced at Honey and I didn't shrug so she did it for me. I gestured to the girl trussed up on the bed.

"Don't mention it," I said. "I'm just glad you were coming back to let the girl you replaced go before you skedaddled with the goods. Or at least I hope you were going to let her go." Then I looked at the boy with the gun and the hair. "Only you got here first."

The singer smiled. He flicked the barrel of his gun more or less in Honey's direction. "We've been watching her for several days. She's a sly one. Smart too. Only we're smarter. Finding this place was a doddle."

My eyebrow was itching to go up but it wouldn't move no matter how much I tried, so I let a few circuits fizz instead.

The singer from the band reached for the jewelry box. He held it up and then he smiled. "We've invested a lot of time and money in acquiring this little box." He held it up in case I didn't know what box he was talking about. "Inside is the key to the whole of the west coast. It'll put us ahead by months, if not *years*."

I nodded. "I get it. Nice little shortcut. With that box you can just move right in. The work has been done for you and your hands are clean. And I can understand why you wanted to steal it rather than buy it. Moving your boys in from across the pond is a big operation. Like you said, it's already cost you time and money. So why not just take the box? Easy, especially if you know that somebody else is planning to grab it. All you gotta do is let them do the hard bit and steal it from the auction, and then you can steal it from the thief. As criminal enterprises go, I'm impressed by the simplicity of it."

The singer gave a laugh that was more an exhalation, like he was apologizing for serving the wrong vintage at his country house garden party.

"Whoever—*whatever*—you are, I like you."

"You weren't too bad yourself," I said. "Your way in was inventive. Pretend to be a beat group and you're right in the middle of it. You boys even had a little fun while you were at it. What did you do? Go around your hideout back in London asking who knew their way around a glockenspiel? I have to say you boys weren't bad, but you won't see my review in tomorrow's paper. I'd take my hat off to you but I'm afraid you might fill it full of holes."

The singer showed me his tonsils. Maybe that was how English people laughed. "Any monkey can learn three chords and hold a note. You Americans are so infatuated with us you'll hire anyone with long hair and an accent to stand on a stage and make a noise. Now, I like you, and I'm sorry it had to end like this, but you do rather talk a little too much."

The others hadn't moved a single muscle and neither had I. I frowned but the guy couldn't see it. I still had the briefcase in my hand. I glanced at the girl on the bed and she looked back at me with eyes that were wide and wet above the gag that was pulled tight between her teeth. Beside the bed the singer chuckled to himself. He put the jewelry box back down on the bed next to the girl. Then he swapped the gun into his other hand. Getting tired of holding it most likely. It was still pointed at Honey but in a less pointed way. His thumb danced over the end of his gun. It was an automatic and there was no hammer to cock but he made the motion anyway. He was getting ready for action.

Honey smiled and she pushed her chin up. This got the singer's attention. He aped the motion with his own chin and I had the feeling he didn't know he was doing it.

"You do this and you'll be making an enemy of Boxer," she said. "He won't make it easy for you. If you expect him to just roll over you've got a screw loose."

The singer did the tonsil thing again. His friends didn't. "My dear," he said. "Mr. Boxer will not be a concern." He waved the end of the gun around the room. "He might have been a kingpin once upon a time, but nobody in this godforsaken city of yours pays him the least bit of attention now. And once everyone else has sworn their fealty to us, it will be Boxer who finds himself in something of a sticky situation, not us."

He raised his gun. He jerked his head at his friends. They got the message. So did I.

I laughed. It sounded like the gears in my Buick slipping.

The singer's expression flickered like a dying lightbulb. I ignored him and nodded at the girl on the mattress. "In a few seconds you're going to want to roll off the bed and, if you can manage it, roll under it."

The girl looked at me with those wide eyes and then after a million years she nodded and while she was nodding the singer looked at her and he looked at me and he looked at Honey.

Then he looked at his friends.

"Kill them."

I don't know what they expected to happen. They were good at their jobs but they weren't perfect and they had overlooked something.

They had overlooked me.

More specifically, they had overlooked the fact that I was six feet and plenty of change and some more again across the middle and all of it was bronzed titanium steel alloy and that *"kill them"* didn't really apply to me on account of the fact that bullets didn't really apply to me either.

I could see how they'd made a mistake. They couldn't have foreseen that the only robot left in the world was going to get in their way. Maybe they hadn't had robots in Merry Olde England. I didn't know. I didn't seem to have that information anywhere in my permanent store.

While I thought about that I saw the girl on the bed roll off it with a muffled whimper followed by a thud as she hit the moldy carpet. As she disappeared over the edge and as the boys were adjusting their grips on their guns I stepped forward while sweeping out with the arm that was holding the briefcase. That arm caught Honey and shoved her backward and then behind me. I felt her grab the briefcase and hold it against herself as I stepped right in front of her. She was much smaller than I was and she knew when to keep her head down.

The Hit List opened up. They had a lot of bullets to fire. The air was filled with flying lead and then it was filled with strips of fabric and bits of plaster as the fusillade tore up my coat and my suit and my shirt underneath and sent them ricocheting all over the room. They kept firing even when the window broke and the big sagging landscape picture above the bed fell down and white grit snowed from the ceiling. They kept firing even when one of the boys jerked once then fell backward. It all happened to a soundtrack of cracks and bangs and pings. Somewhere behind me Honey was curled into a little ball. She was happy to let me do the talking now. I couldn't see the tied-up girl but I hoped she was safe behind the bed or underneath it.

I counted the shots and did the math and I hoped I'd gotten it right.

I had.

The four men left standing dropped one set of guns and in unison reached behind their own backs to pull their backup pieces from the waistbands of their shiny tailored trousers.

I was a big robot but it was a mistake to confuse size and speed. I was big but I wasn't slow.

The backup pieces were never fired and when I was done the Hit List were not going to be making sweet music ever again.

I left the motel room and I pulled the briefcase and Honey and the other girl from under the bed with me. Honey had the jewelry box in one hand. Out in the parking lot Honey untied the girl and I opened the briefcase and fished out a few notes. I pressed them into the girl's hand and told her to run and keep running until she was outside the city limits.

Honey and I watched her until she disappeared around a corner and then I turned to Honey.

"Get in the car," I said, and she did.

And so did I.

13

"They'll find out what happened," Honey said. "By now all the syndicates on the Pacific coast will be looking for the box, and eventually someone will find the bodies."

We looked down on the city. We were up high. By the Hollywood sign. The sun was coming up. The sign was lit by four thousand lightbulbs. I counted them twice. I had a feeling the lightbulbs were new. I had a feeling I'd been up here not too long ago.

Then that feeling began to evaporate like the early morning fog that clung to the city below us.

We'd headed out of the old motel parking lot in a hurry. The place was empty but the gunfire had been very loud. Someone was going to call someone.

Honey left the destination to me. We hadn't spoken on the drive. All I wanted to do was get some distance and find somewhere nice and quiet where Honey and I could be alone. The hills seemed like a good idea. I don't know why I was drawn to the sign but I was. There was an access road behind the sign and a parking lot that was just a dirt platform cut into the hill. There was a hut there and nothing else. Parks Department most likely. Then we got out of the car. Then I pulled off the scraps of my trench coat. The suit jacket underneath was also finished but it was still hanging together so I left it where it was. We took a walk. I led the way. I didn't know where I was going. Honey followed. Now we were here. Looking down on the city as it woke up.

Forty minutes left. It would take twenty minutes to get back to the office. More in the traffic that was starting to build.

"They'll find the bodies, but they won't find the box," I said. I turned from the view to the girl. "That doesn't help your father much. As soon as you hand the box over and he gets to work, they'll know he has it, and they'll know how he got it. And I don't think anyone is going to like that much."

Honey didn't say anything. She was cold. I could tell. She had her arms wrapped around her shoulders, but that wasn't doing much. She wasn't dressed for a hike.

I pursed my lips and enjoyed the way that made the charge fluctuate in a circuit. I turned back to the view. It was quite something and I knew I wouldn't remember it so I wanted to look at it for as long as I could.

"Unless Bob really was the only one of those hoods who could identify you," I said. "So maybe you and your dad will be okay. They'll find the bodies but not the box and they'll never be able to put the picture together. Those British boys seemed to be the only ones who thought to keep an eye on the exiled Mr. Boxer. And that girl, she doesn't know anything either. She's just a dancer for hire who I suspect will be looking for a new job by breakfast."

I turned and looked up at the towering letters above me. They were very high. You could fall to your death from the top of the O, you really could.

Honey and I hadn't spoken on the drive up the hill but the telephone had rung. I'd picked up the receiver and I put it down again. Then I'd slid it off the cradle so it wouldn't ring again. I knew who was calling but I wasn't in the mood for talking.

Not just yet. I was still going over my notes.

"If you don't work for Boxer, then who do you work for?" asked Honey. She squinted in the morning light and looked sideways at me. I looked back at her. I could see it in her face. She'd seen what I'd done in the motel room. "The way you're talking, it sounds like you don't want what's in the box." Her eyes lingered on my optics for a moment and then turned back to the view. "It was my mistake at the club, to think that Father Dearest had sent you," she said. "So what were you doing there, anyway?"

I looked at her. She looked at me.

"I was there to kill you," I said.

Honey's eyes narrowed. I wasn't sure if she was receiving me because she said "Okay" slowly and kept those narrow eyes pointing right at me.

"A robot assassin, huh?" She smiled. "Like I said, my mistake. So who sent you?"

"I don't know. You were in a room full of mobsters. Could have been any of them. Could have been none of them. Maybe it was someone who wasn't invited and who wanted to spoil the party. Maybe it was someone with a beef against your dad and the perfect idea to get even. Maybe someone you've crossed paths with in your line of work who didn't appreciate it."

Honey shook her head. "The path we take, huh?"

I turned back to the view and thought about those words. The path we take. Perhaps. Yes, I was a professional, but not by my choice, by *Ada's*. She'd changed my program and had only told me when I'd worked out what was going on for myself.

Maybe I was no different from Honey. She was a hood, like the others in that club. Organized crime was a family business. She'd been born into it. That was all she had ever known.

So did that mean she had a choice? Or was she destined or doomed to follow a path that had been chosen for her?

The path we take.

I'd been mulling a choice in my mind. I sent it down the positive flux diodes on my left side and kicked it up the negative return resistors on my right.

I looked out across the city. I adjusted my focus. I was trying to see my office from the hillside. I wasn't sure I was looking in the right place. "You were wrong," I said.

Honey huffed in the cold morning air. "About what?"

"The box. The mysterious something. The key to it all. I do want it. I think my boss will find it useful."

Honey's face did something strange. Her eyes went wide and she smiled and then the smile vanished and her eyes narrowed again. She dropped her arms back to her sides.

"So you do work for someone? The person on the telephone."

"We all work for someone," I said, "whether we like it or not, whether that was the path we chose or had it chosen for us."

"You can't take it," said Honey. "I went to a lot of trouble to get it. It's important to us. It belongs to us now. There's too much riding on it to let you take it."

Inside my head I pursed my lips.

Honey turned back to the sunrise. She laughed. It was that old laugh. Loud and long. It echoed around the Hollywood sign and it echoed around the hillside and I thought early morning dog walkers out at the Griffith

Observatory could probably hear it.

Then Honey shook her head and turned around and she headed back up the path to the parking lot and to the access road. "It was fun," she said. "I'll call you sometime."

I listened to her footsteps crunch on the dirt and the gravel. They got fainter and fainter, but they were still there.

I checked my clock.

I had thirty minutes left and I had a job to do.

I turned and walked up the hill after her.

14

I eased back into the alcove in the computer room that was behind my office. Lights flashed all around me. I was back inside Ada with two minutes to go before my tape ran out.

Two minutes before my world ended and I forgot about my troubles. Two minutes before the tape stopped and I began to recharge and then I would wake up with a fresh tape and a clean slate.

I decided that this was no bad thing. I was still thinking about what Honey had said. The path we take. They were just four words but they carried a weight and a meaning. I thought about them and I thought about Honey as I unbuttoned the remains of my shirt and popped my chest panel, the panel that was new and shiny and curved and that didn't sit quite right. I thought about Honey and where I'd left her as I plugged in the power cable and counted the seconds in my head.

"I gotta admit, Ray, you were cutting it mighty close there."

Ada blew smoke around my circuits. Or at least I

thought she did. She was all around me. Her tapes were spinning. Her lights were flashing.

The computer room had a table and a chair in the middle of it. On the table was the early morning edition of the newspaper and my hat. It was the only part of my wardrobe that had remained untouched.

But that was okay. I could afford a new suit. Because next to the hat was the case of Falzarano's money. Ada had clucked over it like a mother hen. I'd been right. It had softened the pain a little.

"Good job, chief," she said.

I didn't say anything. On the computer bank to my right the two big reel-to-reel tapes skidded to a halt then reversed direction. The magnetic tape looped out a little then snapped back to full tension.

"Something on your mind?" Ada asked. Maybe she sighed. Maybe she didn't.

"A few things, Ada, yes," I said.

Another puff of an imaginary cigarette.

One minute until lights out.

"You did good, Ray," she said. "You can trust me on this one. Not only did you do the job and snag a nice bonus, but you might just have filled those gaps in my memory banks, too."

Next to the case on the table was something else. A small wooden jewelry box. It was open, revealing a red velvet cushion, on which sat the prize half the crime syndicates in the country wanted to get their hands on.

It was a key, small and silvery, nothing special. It had no markings, no engravings. It looked like any kind of key, maybe one to a padlock or a cupboard.

Or, according to the card of instructions that had been sitting under the lid of the box, a safety deposit box, inside of which were the full records of the Gray Lake syndicate, a criminal organization wiped out not by the LAPD or the FBI but by the passage of time, the last, heirless don preparing a tasty little inheritance for his rivals to fight over. Because inside the safety deposit box was everything from bank accounts to log books, property deeds, contact lists and address books, ledgers and accounts for gambling, protection, money laundering, and a dozen other crimes that generated large profits and that would enable another enterprise to move right in and take over half the crime in the city and the profits thereof in the blink of an eye.

For a million and change, it was a bargain. And for us, a useful cache. There was enough locked away in a vault on the other side of the city to give Ada all the information about the city's underworld she could possibly want, along with a healthy amount of pocket money and a useful list of contacts.

Behind the table was the big window. Although the

daylight was growing, the window overlooked the brown brick of the building opposite and I could still see my own reflection in the glass. I looked at the grill of my mouth. The sharp triangle of my nose. The round glass eyes that glowed a faint yellow.

"The path we take," I said.

Ada tutted. "Time to go to bed, Ray."

I looked up at the ceiling into the corner. There was no lens there but I knew Ada could see me and I thought that was more or less where she could see me from.

"Goodnight, Ray. Sweet dreams."

I heard the ticking of a watch. A stopwatch, the second hand racing to oblivion.

And then I woke up on another beautiful morning in Hollywood, California.

About the Author

Photograph by Lou Abercrombie

ADAM CHRISTOPHER is a novelist, comic book writer, and award-winning editor. The author of *Seven Wonders, The Age Atomic,* and *Hang Wire,* and cowriter of *The Shield* for Dark Circle Comics, Adam has also written novels based on the hit CBS television show *Elementary.* His debut novel, *Empire State,* was *SciFi-Now*'s Book of the Year and a *Financial Times* Book of the Year for 2012. Born in New Zealand, Adam has lived in Great Britain since 2006. Find him online at www.adamchristopher.co.uk and on Twitter as @ghostfinder.

TOR·COM

Science fiction. Fantasy. The universe.

And related subjects.

*

More than just a publisher's website, *Tor.com* is a venue for **original fiction, comics,** and **discussion** of the entire field of SF and fantasy, in all media and from all sources. Visit our site today — and join the conversation yourself.